The Billionaire's Deception

by

Shawna Delacorte

The Billionaire's Deception

Cover Art by *Diana Carlile*

The Wild Rose Press, Inc.
PO Box 708
Adams Basin, NY 14410-0708

Publishing History
First Edition, 2022
Trade Paperback ISBN 978-1-5092-4500-0
Digital ISBN 978-1-5092-4501-7

Published in the United States of America

**Will an innocent deception
create a chasm too large to cross?**

She grabbed the rickety, old wooden stepladder and placed it below the shelf. Steadying herself with one hand against the wall, she climbed up four steps. *I should have listened to Mike about buying a new ladder.* As she cautiously reached for the carton, she heard the front door open and close.

"Is that you, Mike? I could sure use some help in here."

Cassie stood a petite five feet three inches, not quite tall enough to reach the carton. She tentatively climbed one more step to the top of the ladder. With both arms stretched above her head, she tried to coax the box off the shelf with her fingertips.

The unstable old ladder swayed and shook. Her heartbeat jumped into high gear. Panic shoved hard at her. She desperately tried to grab something, anything to keep from falling. Almost like a slow-motion scene in a movie, she felt the ladder give way and went tumbling backward out of control.

Shock jolted through her as a pair of strong arms caught her, followed by the sound of an unfamiliar voice—a smooth, sexy male voice. "Mike doesn't seem to be here. Will I do?"

Chapter One

"Cassie, honey, could I have a refill?" The ruddy-faced fisherman in his late fifties held up his cup. Cassie Brockton immediately grabbed the coffee pot and filled the empty mug.

"You're in luck, Jake." She flashed a warm, open smile. "It's a freshly brewed pot." The typical early morning breakfast—locals, no tourists—boasted an open and friendly atmosphere in the restaurant. Everyone knew everyone. No one had any secrets. It still amazed her when she thought of how easily she had adapted to the lifestyle on the island and how quickly the locals had accepted an outsider.

Fate worked in such strange ways. One year ago, she lived in Chicago, newly divorced after a year of bitter arguments and legal battles. She had just been promoted to vice president at a large banking concern, the youngest woman to achieve that position. Unfortunately, the promotion included a high dose of stress accompanied by a borderline case of burnout. And all of that at the age of only thirty-four.

Then the letter arrived, the one that changed her entire life. To her surprise, she had been named as sole heir to her Aunt Sofie's estate—a small restaurant and bar in the San Juan Islands just off the Washington State mainland.

"I don't know what you do to the coffee—" Jake's

robust laugh filled the air. "—but it's a definite improvement over what Sofie used to serve."

Cassie reached across the counter and gave a friendly pat to his potbelly. "You old teddy bear. Flattery like that will not get you a free breakfast, so stop trying." She dearly adored Jake. From her first day on the island, he had taken her under his wing. He had helped her adjust and fit in with her new surroundings and lifestyle. She had lost both of her parents shortly after graduating from college. Jake had been a father figure for her from the day she arrived to take possession of her inheritance.

He drained the last of the coffee from his cup and tossed some money on the counter. "I'll see you later, Cassie." He paused to exchange a few words with almost everyone on his way out.

The next two hours continued to be very busy with a constant stream of customers—all hungry. The rush finally settled down, the last customer of the morning on the way out the door. She took advantage of the lull to restock some supplies and get ready for the lunch crowd.

"Berta," she called into the kitchen, "now would be a good time for you and Danny to go to the store. We're running low on a few items, and it's a couple of days before our weekly supply order is delivered."

The plump woman in her early fifties with the warm, open face wiped her hands on her apron as she walked out of the kitchen. "Whew! That was quite a breakfast rush." Her tone was cheery and upbeat. "For a while there, I had the entire grill covered with eggs, bacon, sausage, hash browns, and had three omelets working all at the same time."

Berta offered a good-natured laugh. "I was about ready to call for a time-out. If it hadn't been for Danny giving me a hand, you'd still have customers waiting for food. Everyone in town must have decided to eat breakfast here this morning instead of home."

Cassie looked around the restaurant. "Where's Danny now?" She peered through the door leading to the kitchen.

"He finally caught up with the dishes, and now he's taking out the trash. Your decision to install an automatic dishwasher a few months ago has certainly been a blessing. It's freed up some of Danny's time so he can help me."

"How's he doing as the *assistant chef*?"

Berta gave an amused chuckle. "If you're asking how he's doing as the *cook's helper*, I'm very pleased. He's conscientious about his duties. We might have the makings of a real cook on our hands."

Her brow furrowed in thought. "If I take Danny with me, you'll be here all alone. We'll be gone half an hour, maybe a little longer."

"I'll be just fine. Mike should be here in ten or fifteen minutes to start setting up the bar before lunch. If I run into a sudden rush, he can give me a hand."

Berta untied her apron and laid it aside. "We'll be back as soon as we can." She hurried through the kitchen and out the back door.

Cassie continued to refill salt and pepper shakers, sugar jars, and napkin holders. Before she had finished, she ran out of napkins. She searched the cartons on the floor of the storeroom, but to no avail. She surveyed the shelves, then her gaze landed on the sought-after carton sitting on the top shelf in the storage room. *Who put something in constant use way up there?*

She grabbed the rickety, old wooden stepladder and placed it below the shelf. Steadying herself with one hand against the wall, she climbed up four steps. *I should have listened to Mike about buying a new ladder.* As she cautiously reached for the carton, she heard the front door open and close.

"Is that you, Mike? I could sure use some help in here."

Cassie stood a petite five feet three inches, not quite tall enough to reach the carton. She tentatively climbed one more step to the top of the ladder. With both arms stretched above her head, she tried to coax the box off the shelf with her fingertips.

The unstable old ladder swayed and shook. Her heartbeat jumped into high gear. Panic shoved hard at her. She desperately tried to grab something, anything to keep from falling. Almost like a slow-motion scene in a movie, she felt the ladder give way and went tumbling backward out of control.

Shock jolted through her as a pair of strong arms caught her, followed by the sound of an unfamiliar voice—a smooth, sexy male voice. "Mike doesn't seem to be here. Will I do?"

She instinctively wrapped her arms around her rescuer's neck and clung tightly to him. Her erratic breathing matched the way her heart pounded in her chest. She tried to force her breathing under control. As her panic subsided, she turned her head and looked into sky blue eyes that twinkled with amusement...and a hint of something else. Something much more personal.

A quick intake of breath darted through her, followed by a not so subtle tingle of excitement. His taut, muscular body and tanned good looks grabbed her immediate attention.

"What's going on here?" She turned toward the sound of the familiar voice belonging to the stocky, fifty-five-year-old bartender standing in the doorway. "Cassie, are you okay?"

Quickly regaining her composure, she removed her arms from around the stranger's neck. "I'm fine, Mike, thanks to this gentleman. He caught me in the nick of time, just before I hit the floor. I was trying to reach a carton of napkins on the top shelf and fell." She allowed a self-conscious chuckle in an attempt to cover her mortification. "You were right. I definitely need to replace this old stepladder."

The stranger's smile mesmerized her, sending unexpected little tremors through her body. He continued to hold her, making no effort to put her down. A heated flush of embarrassment burned across her cheeks. She lowered her eyelids, her gaze landing on the floor. "I...I believe you can put me down now."

"Oh, yeah." His voice teased her as he carried her out of the storage room into the restaurant and set her on a counter stool. "I didn't realize I still had hold of you."

Mike carefully eyed the stranger, a look of caution and disapproval covering his face. "Are you sure everything's okay here, Cassie?"

"Everything's fine. Go on and set up the bar." Mike still seemed reticent about leaving her alone with the stranger. He looked toward the kitchen. "Where's Berta and Danny?"

"They went to the store. We had such a rush this morning that we ran low on some items, so I thought we should stock up during the lull before lunch. It's two more days before our regular supply delivery."

Mike shot a harsh glare at the stranger, then unlocked and opened the pocket door separating the bar from the restaurant. He leveled one last look of warning at the stranger, then addressed Cassie. "I'll be right here if you need me."

Then he disappeared into the other room, the meaning of his glare and tone of voice clearly evident. The sounds of bottles and glasses being moved around reached her ears as Mike readied the bar for lunch business.

Cassie turned her attention toward the man who had saved her. "Thanks for coming to my rescue. I'd hate to think what might have happened if you hadn't been there." She smiled warmly and extended her hand. "I'm Cassie Brockton."

He grasped her hand and returned her smile. "Trent Nichols. It was my pleasure. Rescuing damsels in distress is my specialty."

She took a moment to carefully scrutinize him. He was even better looking than she had first thought. He stood just a little under six feet, probably five feet ten inches. He had a youthful appearance even with the little wrinkles at the corners of his eyes. He needed a haircut, but she could tell his dark blond hair with the sun bleached streaks had once been a very stylish cut. She guessed his age to be about forty, maybe a year or two younger.

He seemed to be well-groomed in spite of his shaggy hair. His faded and worn jeans had a couple of holes in the knees, and his T-shirt looked old, but the garments were clean. "I've never seen you before. Are you new on the island?"

"Yes, I just arrived."

She glanced out the window and saw the Washington State Ferry pulling away from the dock. "So I see."

Trent Nichols found her statement confusing until he turned and followed her line of sight to the ferryboat. He started to correct her but caught himself and allowed her incorrect assumption to stand rather than admit that he arrived on his yacht. Discretion became the word of the day until he had time to accurately assess the situation. The less said to the locals, the better. "This is the first restaurant I saw, so here I am."

Cassie jumped up and hurried behind the counter. "You're probably wanting some coffee." She grabbed the pot, looked at it, then quickly set it aside. Picking up a clean pot, she shoved it into the machine and pressed the button. "That stuff is pretty old. In fact, it's so strong it could probably serve itself. I'll have a fresh pot in a couple of minutes. Meanwhile"—she grabbed a menu and handed it to him—"you can look over the selections. We start our switch over to the lunch menu in about ten minutes if you'd like to wait, but breakfast items are still available."

He took the menu from her. "I was just next door at the motel—"

"I'm sorry, but Bob Hampton has misled you." Her clipped words had a sharp edge to them. Anger darted across her face as her green eyes darkened and narrowed. The sudden change in her demeanor caught him completely off guard. "This restaurant is a separate business from the motel. There are no provisions for his guests to charge meals to their room and pay for them at the motel when they check out. I hope this doesn't inconvenience you."

"Whoa!" He threw up his hands in a defensive posture as he registered surprise at Cassie's sudden and unexpected verbal attack. "I was going to say I had just been next door and was surprised to find the motel closed. Even if it's only a seasonal business, it seems that it should be open by now."

The crimson flush of embarrassment spread across her cheeks as she glanced at the floor. "I'm sorry. It's just that...well, uh...I obviously made a wrong assumption. Please accept my apology." She offered a shy smile.

"No harm done." He extended a smile that said he had dismissed the matter from his mind, a reality far from the truth.

He hadn't anticipated anything like this when he walked up the ramp from the harbor located next to the ferry dock. He had stopped at the top of the ramp to get his bearings. The main street of the town ran in front of him, parallel to the coast line. He had spotted the object of his search across the street—the *Harbor View Motel.*

The island had not been one of his planned stops, but he had promised to do a favor for Randall Davies, a Seattle attorney and longtime friend. Randall had received a letter from a man named Bob Hampton who said he had inherited a large parcel of land six months ago, including a motel, with a restaurant and bar next door and a house behind the restaurant. Hampton had asked Randall to represent him but hadn't said what he wanted to accomplish or why he needed an attorney.

The letter had been disturbingly vague. Randall had never met Bob Hampton nor seen the property and wasn't sure exactly why the man had contacted him. It made more sense for Hampton to use the attorney who handled the inheritance and would have been familiar with the property.

Randall confided to Trent that his first inclination had been to dismiss the letter and refuse to accept this potential client. Since Trent already planned to pilot his yacht through the San Juan Islands headed for Canada, Randall had asked him if he would do a cursory check of the situation.

Trent had crossed the street to the motel. The *Closed* sign on the door had caught him by surprise. Very odd. Even if only a seasonal business, being the first week of May with the Memorial Day holiday weekend approaching, the motel should have been open for the summer season, or at least showing signs of preparing to open. A quick inspection of the outside of the building showed a definite need for repairs, but it appeared to be primarily cosmetic refurbishing rather than structural damage. Trent's overall first impression of the situation? Not favorable.

Expanding, updating the facilities, and adding resort type amenities such as a spa, pool, and exercise room would be in order. There seemed to be ample parking and plenty of vacant land available, assuming the surrounding land belonged with the motel. He needed to get a look inside before forming any more of an opinion.

It had again struck him as odd. A prime location on the main street of town right across from the ferry dock and harbor, no other motel in the immediate vicinity, it should be a profitable operation that could sustain a year-round clientele. He had glanced next door toward

Sofie's Coffee Pot and the *Main Street Tavern*, apparently the restaurant and bar mentioned in the letter. At least the restaurant had an *Open* sign on the door. He had hoped that someone there could tell him where to locate the owner of the property.

He wrinkled his brow in a moment of thought. It had now become obvious that the matter required more investigation than either he or Randall Davies had originally thought. He needed to stick around for a while to get an accurate evaluation, at least until he could talk to Bob Hampton and straighten out the confusion.

He turned his attention to Cassie, watching as she gathered a coffee mug, glass of water, and a place setting of eating utensils wrapped in a napkin. He opened the menu. Then a sudden realization hit him. *Oh, damn.* He jammed his hand into his pocket and withdrew some coins and a one dollar bill. Irritation jabbed at him as he shoved the money back in his pocket then closed the menu. He had forgotten to grab his wallet when he left his yacht to come ashore.

When he had made the decision to allow her to think he had arrived on the ferry, he had done it to keep from creating any suspicions until he had control of the situation. The ferry seemed less *outsider* than to admit he had arrived on his own boat—a sixty-foot power yacht with three bedrooms that could comfortably sleep six people.

A little sigh of resignation escaped his throat. He wasn't that hungry, anyway. He had only stopped at the harbor to carry out the promised favor for Randall, a business deal in which he had no personal interest. He originally thought it would only take an hour or two of his time. Another sigh escaped into the open. Obviously, he had been wrong.

Trent shifted his attention as he studied the delightful young woman who had fallen so unexpectedly into his arms. Her petite size and short, blonde hair had initially made her seem more cute than anything else. As he studied her, he realized she was not just cute. He took in the way her jeans hugged her hips and legs, accentuating a delightfully rounded bottom and trim waist. Her sunny yellow blouse managed to convey some rather enticing curves without being low cut or too tight. Her bright green eyes sparkled when she talked. Her finely sculpted features created a truly lovely face—a beautiful face.

Definitely more than merely *cute*.

The man closed the menu after checking his money. Cassie placed the coffee mug, glass of water, and silverware in front of him, then grabbed the pot of freshly brewed coffee and filled his cup. "What would you like to eat?"

"Nothing to eat, thanks. Just the coffee will be fine." He took a sip, then flashed a dazzling yet sincere smile. "Good and hot."

So obvious—frayed clothing, his need of a haircut, the way he checked his money, then closed the menu— he could not afford to buy breakfast. She appreciated and respected the fact that he did not try to con her out of a meal, did not eat, then suddenly discover he had left his wallet in his other pants.

He didn't exhibit the type of behavior she associated with her life in Chicago, the type of negative thing she thought most people would have done. And he didn't even make mention of the fact that she certainly owed him something for literally saving her neck.

She projected an outgoing, teasing attitude, not wanting to embarrass him, at least, not any more than she probably already had with her unwarranted harsh comment about him staying at the motel. "That will never do. If it weren't for you, I'd surely have broken something, possibly several somethings. Maybe even something important. The very least I can do is show my appreciation by treating you to breakfast." She took her order pad and pencil from her apron pocket and extended a friendly smile. "Now, how do you like your eggs?"

Trent found her utterly enchanting. Her smile captivated him. Perhaps this island would be a good place to stay for a couple of days after he concluded his business commitment to Randall. He had no particular plan or itinerary in mind when he'd wrapped up all his own pressing business matters in Beverly Hills and told his law partner he had decided to take off for about three months. He needed to get his head together, to get away from the Los Angeles rat race. The stress and pressure associated with his high-profile Beverly Hills law firm had gotten to him the last several months. He had experienced all the signs of career burnout. He needed a change of scenery. He needed to simplify his life and get back to basics.

Upon graduating top of his class from Harvard law school, he had set a goal of being at least a multi-millionaire well on his way to billionaire, by the age of forty. Through hard work, shrewd investments, and some good luck, he had long ago completed that goal, and he was still a year away from that fortieth birthday.

Granted, a few of his investments had been the result of insider information from clients, but nothing that hurt anyone else or had a negative impact on the market or the company where he had invested his money.

Now, however, it seemed he no longer had any purpose to his life. His work no longer excited him the way it used to. The public social whirl had also become more of a tedious burden than a pleasure. He had grown tired of the endless string of status-seeking women. He wanted to settle down with someone genuine, someone with her feet firmly planted in reality. Unfortunately, he didn't know anyone like that nor did he know how to go about finding that special someone. At least not in the world where he functioned on a daily basis.

He returned his thoughts to her question. "I couldn't possibly allow you to cover the cost of my breakfast." He felt a little sheepish as he started to explain that he didn't have his wallet on him at the moment but could certainly afford to pay for his meal.

She lowered her voice slightly and leaned toward him even though no one could hear her. "Look, I saw you check your money, then decide not to order. I really do owe you for saving me from that fall. Now, I won't hear any more about it. If you don't tell me what you want, I'll just have to guess."

Perhaps he had become jaded over the years. The concept of lending a helping hand to one's fellow man out of the goodness of one's heart was something he hadn't come across in a long time. He donated generously to various charities, but he gave only money without any personal involvement.

He glanced down at his clothes—old and worn although he preferred to think of them as properly broken in and comfortable, and not enough money in his pockets to pay for breakfast. He could certainly understand why she would have made the assumption she did. Cassie Brockton became more and more intriguing with each passing minute.

"How about the specialty of the house—fresh salmon steak, eggs, shepherd's potatoes, fruit compote, and freshly squeezed orange juice."

"Sounds like a complete banquet, but I'm really not that hungry. I think just a couple of scrambled eggs and bacon...and I insist on paying for my breakfast." He took another sip of his coffee as he watched her hurry off toward the kitchen. He would pay her as soon as he retrieved his wallet from the boat. Meanwhile, he would kick back, relax, and enjoy his conversation with this delightful, down-to-earth woman.

He looked around, his practiced gaze taking in everything with a quick sweep of the room. It seemed to be a nice little operation. He wondered exactly how Cassie fit in. She apparently had the authority to offer him a free meal, and Mike had deferred to her instructions to get to work.

She returned from the kitchen with a big glass of orange juice. "Berta should be back any minute, so if you can wait, you'll get a much more enjoyable breakfast than if I cook it myself."

He tried to suppress a grin. "Not much of a hand in the kitchen? Your husband have any problems with that?" His smile faded when a quick flash of anger darted through her eyes, followed closely by a sigh of resignation.

The muscles in her jaw clenched into a taut line. "Not anymore, he doesn't." Her voice held an edge to it, different from the note he had detected when he mentioned being at the motel.

"Hey, I'm sorry. I didn't mean to pry." He leveled a quizzical look at her.

Her face relaxed as she offered him an apologetic smile. "Don't worry about it. It's ancient history." Her brow wrinkled into a frown. "We lived in Chicago. He was a hotshot attorney who considered his exalted career far more important than my *lowly* career in banking."

He heard the anger and resentment in her voice. Her words might have called it *ancient history*, but her tone said the animosity surrounding the situation of her marriage and divorce remained very much alive.

She refilled his coffee cup. "What brings you to the island?"

"Oh, just wandering around, looking for a nice place to spend some time." He had caught the decidedly sharp edge of bitterness when she mentioned *attorney*. What should have been an easy going and open conversation had just become complicated and strained.

No doubt that a definite conflict existed between the motel and the restaurant. Bob Hampton's letter alluded to the fact that he owned it all, but Cassie emphatically stated that no connection existed between the motel and the restaurant. And then, on top of that, this delightful woman very clearly voiced a decidedly negative opinion of his profession.

"What about you?" He cocked his head and gave her a questioning look. "You said you were from Chicago. Have you lived here very long?"

"I inherited this place from my aunt about a year ago and thought I'd try my hand at running it. Things were a little shaky for the first couple of months, but now I feel very comfortable and at home."

"No desire to return to the big city?"

"Absolutely none."

"This must have been quite an adjustment from Chicago."

Her comments confused him. Bob Hampton claimed to have inherited the property six months ago and now Cassie said she inherited this business a year ago. Exactly who owned what?

She laughed, an open, warm laugh. He liked the way her nose crinkled and her eyes sparkled. "*An adjustment* hardly begins to describe it." She cleared away his empty orange juice glass, refilled his coffee cup, then ducked into the kitchen at the sound of the back door. She quickly returned. "Berta is back. She'll have your food ready right away."

A tall, gangly teenage boy of about eighteen appeared from the kitchen, carrying a sack from the store. He went behind the counter and put things away.

Cassie turned toward the teenager. "Danny, could you please finish filling the napkin holders? I got distracted part way through and didn't get it done." She started to say something to Trent, then returned her attention to Danny. "You need to put *stepladder* on the shopping list."

Trent laughed. "You definitely need a new one." He enjoyed his conversation with Cassie despite her definitely negative attitude toward attorneys.

"Well, enough about my carelessness." Once again a pink tinge of embarrassment spread across her cheeks. "Are you planning to stay on the island for a while?"

"When I arrived I hadn't planned on staying,

but…" For the first time, he searched the depths of her eyes looking for… Looking for what? Trying to find answers to questions too long left unasked? Solutions to problems too long left unresolved?

"I think I might like to stay for a while." The spontaneous decision was made only a fraction of a second before the words left his mouth, a decision separate from his business for Randall. "However, the motel seems to be closed. Since I'm without a car, is there somewhere close by where I could get a room?"

Again he found himself torn between his business necessities and his personal needs. He could stay on his boat where he could be very comfortable but decided to not mention it especially since he'd allowed her to assume he had arrived on the ferry.

Cassie's gaze locked with his. Unexpected tremors tried to get a foothold inside her. The pull of his sexual magnetism, almost like a mystical meshing of their souls, refused to let go of her. The memory of being cradled in his arms rebuffed her efforts to shove the sensation aside. He hadn't tried to con her out of a meal and had even objected to the idea of her providing him with a free breakfast. Obviously articulate, his smooth voice was cultured, and his blue eyes sparkled with intelligence.

Cassie searched for something…anything…to dismiss the desires pulling at her senses. "I…uh…I have a spare room I sometimes rent during the summer tourist season." She didn't like the hesitation in her voice but couldn't prevent it. "It has its own entrance to the outside and a private bathroom. It's reasonably priced…" Her breath caught in her throat as she looked into his clear blue eyes. "If, uh, if you'd be interested."

Chapter Two

Trent jumped at the unexpected turn of events and an excellent solution to his problem. That would put him *on the scene*, give him an excuse for being there. He could gather the information Randall needed without arousing suspicions about the true reason for his presence. "That sounds perfect. I'll take it."

With each passing minute, he found himself drawn more and more to Cassie, a personal interest totally separate from any business considerations for Randall Davies. Yes, indeed. This town on this island just might be the ideal place to spend some time away from everything. A place to relax and unwind, to rejuvenate his former zest for life...to give his life that new purpose and direction he had been searching for when he left Beverly Hills.

"I stored my belongings in a locker down at the dock. I'll get my things and be right back...and pay for my breakfast."

As soon as he finished eating, he hurried to his boat and packed what he would need for a couple of weeks, not knowing how long he would be staying. He hadn't realized it at the time, but he appreciated the stroke of good luck that docked his boat out of line-of-sight from Cassie's restaurant. An abstract thought invaded his mind as he put clothes into a duffel bag, a thought that toyed with the idea of staying the entire summer.

A moment of uncertainty grabbed him. He acknowledged his discomfort about deceiving Cassie, but he managed to convince himself it was only a harmless deception and a necessary one in light of her decidedly adverse opinion of the legal profession. No one would be hurt by it. He would take care of his business obligation to Randall as quickly as possible, leaving the rest of his time free to relax and once again be able to indulge the simple joys of everyday life. He might even check into buying a summer house on the island, a place a world away from his *normal* day-to-day existence and a lifestyle that no longer appealed to him.

****

While Trent fetched his things, Cassie apprised her employees of what had happened. "The man who just left to collect his belongings is Trent Nichols. He was looking for a place to stay, and Bob Hampton apparently has the *Closed* sign on the motel entrance"—she rolled her eyes indicating her opinion of Bob—"for reasons only he understands. So…I've rented Trent my spare room."

"Oh, my, this is quite a surprise." Berta voiced her thoughts before anyone else.

Danny registered surprise but in his typical manner didn't say anything.

Mike, on the other hand, had plenty to say. "I'm goin' on record right now. I don't like it. This guy's an outsider, just showed up from out of nowhere."

"He didn't materialize out of thin air…or beam down from a spaceship." Cassie offered a teasing grin in an attempt to placate the always skeptical bartender. "He arrived on the ferry."

A scowl crossed Mike's face. "This guy's a stranger...an outsider. We don't know nothin' about him. Well...almost nothin'." He shot Cassie a stern look of disapproval. "When I arrived for work, I found him in the storage room tryin' to have his way with you."

"That's not true, Mike. I heard the front door open and thought it was you. I called out, saying I needed some help. Then that old ladder heaved a final death rattle and gave way. I fell from the top step, and he caught me. Probably saved me from breaking a bone or two—or worse." Once again, the memory of Trent cradling her in his arms sent a tremor of heated desire rushing through her body.

"Yeah, well, I can't stop you from rentin' him a room, but I'll be keepin' an eye on this guy. Makin' sure he don't take advantage of you...again."

It wasn't that Mike didn't trust Trent specifically. Mike didn't trust much of anyone. It had taken Jake to convince him that Cassie could be trusted. Now he felt as protective of her as Jake did.

Before there could be any more discussion of the matter, Trent entered through the front door carrying a duffel bag. The first thing he did was pay for his breakfast. After introductions were made, Cassie turned toward Mike. "If you could keep an eye on things, I'll get Trent settled into his room, then be right back."

"Yeah...no problem." Mike shot an unmistakable glare of warning toward Trent. "I'll keep my eye on *everything*."

****

Duffel bag in hand, Trent followed Cassie up the path to the old two-story house that sat higher on the hill looking out over the harbor and to the islands beyond. It had a large covered wrap-around porch with an old-fashioned swing. Pots of brightly colored flowers hung from the porch railing. She opened the screen door, and they went inside.

"This is the living room. Across the hall"—she indicated with a wave of her hand—"is the dining room." Even though the furnishings were mostly old pieces, some of them obviously antiques, it all appeared neat and clean. Everything probably came with the house she inherited. It looked as if it had belonged to someone's maiden aunt.

She continued past the staircase toward the back of the house. "There's a kitchen and a half-bath this way." He followed her down the hall to the bright, cheery kitchen with a breakfast nook at one end. The back door led to a small yard with more flowers.

They left the kitchen and went back into the hallway where she unfastened a bolt lock that secured a door from inside the house. "This is the room I have available." She stepped aside and let him enter ahead of her. "Aunt Sofie used to rent the room out to summer tourists. I still do the same…occasionally."

She walked across the room to the door leading out onto the front porch. "This is your entrance. You can use this door to come and go in private. This"—she indicated another door across the room—"is your private bathroom. It has both a tub and a shower."

Trent looked around the large bedroom and glanced into the bathroom. Like the rest of the house, it appeared neat and clean—a large four-poster bed with a nightstand on each side, a dresser, and a chest with a television on top. A comfortable looking easy chair and reading lamp occupied one corner and next to it was a small desk. A full length mirror hung on the closet door.

He extended a warm smile. "This is very nice. I'm sure I'll be comfortable."

The sparkle in the depth of his eyes captivated Cassie. He had a handsome face, and his smile showed a row of perfect white teeth. Sun-bleached streaks highlighted his thick, dark blond hair, the length covering the top of his ears and the back of his neck with errant locks hanging in casual disarray across his forehead. His T-shirt accentuated his broad shoulders and well-tanned, muscular arms. The sensation of being cradled in his arms once again swept over her, filling her with the warmth and sense of security she first experienced the moment she ended up in his embrace, the same strong arms that caught her and held her close when she fell. Her breathing increased along with her heartbeat and pulse rate.

She had never been this impulsive with anyone before, offering a complete stranger a room in her home. She knew nothing about him except that he made her insides tremble in an exciting way that she hadn't experienced in a long time.

Trent deposited his bag in the corner of his room, then followed Cassie back into the house. He glanced toward the staircase. "What's up there?"

"That's my bedroom and bathroom."

The sly sparkle in his eyes sent a heated flush across her cheeks. What was there about this man that continued to instill an uncomfortable sense of embarrassment in her?

"There's a second bedroom up there that I use as

an office," she gestured toward the top of the stairs. "It's where I keep my computer and handle the daily bookkeeping chores for the restaurant and bar. I email information to my accountant for the serious accounting chores and taxes."

"What kind of internet service do you have here?"

"You mean here as in at my house or here on the island?"

"Well...I was referring to internet in general—both, I guess."

"The company that supplies television for the island also handles the internet connection. Personally, I have wifi throughout the house." A bit of a shy smile tugged at the corners of her mouth. "It's so I can use my electronic devices in the kitchen and on the porch swing when the weather is nice, in addition to my office."

"That porch swing looked like a nice place to enjoy a glass of wine and watch the sunset."

She nervously ran her fingers through her hair. Something about his presence and that damnably sexy smile... Suddenly, the walls seemed to close in around her, the room became very crowded, the air almost nonexistent. He had neither said nor done anything improper, nothing that would be considered inappropriate or cause her alarm. Uneasiness jittered through her body.

Just one of those things.

At least that's what she wanted to believe.

"Well..." Her nervousness continued to assault her senses. "I need to get back to work. We have to get ready for the lunch rush. If it's anything like this morning's breakfast crowd, we'll be very busy." She started for the front door with Trent following. "The restaurant opens at five o'clock for breakfast and remains open through lunch. We close at two in the afternoon, and we're closed on Monday. The bar opens at eleven in the morning to accommodate the lunch crowd. Mike usually closes the bar somewhere between eleven o'clock and midnight, depending on the amount of business.

"The restaurant isn't open for dinner, but we do serve some food in the bar at night, mostly cold sandwiches and a few other items that don't require cooking. Berta makes the sandwiches, wraps them, and puts them in the refrigerator before she goes home." A thoughtful look crossed her face. "I've been thinking about getting a microwave for the bar. On one hand, it would be good for business to be able to heat food." She furrowed her brow into a slight frown. "But on the other hand, it would give Mike more work to do and he's all alone."

"You open at five o'clock in the morning, six days a week? That's sure early. Tell me…" He again seemed to be searching her eyes. "Do you open the restaurant in the morning, work there all day, then close the bar at night? If so, that's an incredibly long day. It certainly doesn't leave you any time for a social life…" He reached out and gently brushed his fingertips across her cheek sending a little ripple of excitement across her skin. "Or time for yourself."

Something in his eyes—Cassie did not know what—told her his words were meant more for himself than her. She detected a note, just a hint of sadness in those words. Trent Nichols had become a much more complex man than she first thought. But she had also thought him to be down on his luck without enough money to pay for his breakfast. He had been true to his word. He paid for his meal when he returned with his duffel bag.

His unwavering gaze made her uncomfortable. The feel of his fingertips against her skin sent a tremor racing through her body. She turned away and walked out to the porch. "I don't put in that long a day too often. Charlene opens up with Berta. I come in around six thirty when the breakfast rush picks up. I usually take care of the bookkeeping for that day's business and the bar from the night before along with any other business I have when I close the restaurant following lunch. Sometimes I check on the bar during the late afternoon and early evening and help out with happy hour if things are particularly busy, but Mike usually has everything well in hand."

She directed a shy smile toward him. "You happened to catch us while Charlene is in Tacoma tending to her sick mother. She should be back in a few days. In the meantime, it's left us a little shorthanded. It was certainly lucky for me that you showed up when you did." Her gaze dropped to the ground as that pesky flush of embarrassment hit her again. Her voice dropped to just above a whisper. "If you hadn't saved me from that fall, I don't know what we would have done about being open."

Shyness and embarrassment had plagued her from the moment he caught her in his arms even though the words *shy* and *retiring* wouldn't normally apply to her. In fact, it represented an area where she and Jerry, her ex-husband, had ongoing confrontations. He wanted a quiet, stay-at-home wife who would always have dinner waiting for him no matter how late he stayed out—or with whom. She wanted her own career and a husband who treated her with respect and as an equal.

She had no proof of multiple infidelities, but she firmly believed he had been unfaithful to her on numerous occasions and with several different women. One she knew for a fact. She had caught him in bed with a woman—in her own house in their shared bed—when she had returned early from an out-of-town business conference. He had reluctantly admitted to an ongoing affair with the law clerk who worked in his office.

A quick stab of disgust poked at her. Lying, cheating, deceitful attorneys—none of them could be trusted. She hated the lies most of all, the purposeful deceptions, even more than his constant criticism of her decision to pursue a career of her own. In retrospect, she wondered why they had ever gotten married. Or for that matter, why she thought she had been in love with him.

"I'm glad fate decided to intervene and direct me here in time to catch you."

Trent's warm smile and his words, edged with an obvious sincerity, snapped her out of her moment of reflection and brought her back into the present. "Yes, well…" She nervously ran her fingers through her hair again. "I'd better get back to work."

Before she returned to the restaurant, Cassie gave Trent a key to his private outside entrance from the porch and bolted the door to his room from inside the house, thus securing the room from the rest of her living quarters.

****

Trent unpacked and settled into his new surroundings. After turning on his laptop computer, he verified access to Cassie's wifi. Even though her wifi was not password protected, he had security on his laptop to protect its contents when using public access. He also brought a tablet with him when he left home but decided to leave it on his boat as the laptop offered him more work options. After making a file on Randall Davies' project, he entered notes concerning the conflicting information about ownership of the businesses involved and Cassie's reaction to Bob Hampton and the motel.

Now that he had decided to stay and procured a room, he had several details to handle. He made a to-do list for the afternoon. First on the list, a discussion with the harbor master. He decided to pay one month in advance for docking space, an extra service charge to cover security and maintenance, plus a healthy tip for the harbor master's discretion in keeping the identity of the yacht's owner confidential.

Next, he called Grace Edwards, his administrative assistant at his law firm in Beverly Hills. "I'm stopping in the San Juan Islands off the Washington coast for a few days. Unless it's an emergency, only communicate with me through email. I don't want to deal with or need to explain a constantly ringing cell phone or a stream of incoming tweets."

"Why the sudden change of plans? I thought you were headed toward Canada."

"Randall Davies asked me to stop off and do a favor for him. Turns out it's more complex than either of us thought. So...here I am for the time being."

He terminated his call with Grace, but before

tackling his to-do list, he called Randall Davies in Seattle. "I'm not sure what's going on, but the motel is closed and no one knows where Bob Hampton is. My initial inspection of the outside of the building revealed a definite need for refurbishing. But more to the point, there's some confusion about exactly who owns what. Cassie Brockton claims to own the restaurant, bar, and the house. She is emphatic that there is no connection between her business and the motel next door. She says she inherited the bar, restaurant, and house from her aunt a year ago."

"Well, that certainly puts the entire situation in a new light."

"I agree. If you need to reply to his letter right away, I think turning him down is the most practical course of action for you. There are just too many extenuating circumstances and questionable areas, especially with Hampton not being available to straighten out the confusion. I plan to stay a little longer and will check into it further. I'll let you know what else I find. I still intend to talk to Hampton when he shows up. If you need me in the interim, you can reach me with email and in an emergency on my cell."

They talked for another couple of minutes before ending their conversation. Trent took a moment to collect his thoughts. The business, as he perceived its operation, could be a profitable investment. If Bob Hampton wanted to sell the property, he might be interested in taking it off Bob's hands for the right price. Besides, he found Cassie Brockton to be a delightful diversion to his wanderings and his search for…what? Although still unsure about exactly what he was seeking, he had discovered one important thing. He wanted to know more about Cassie. A lot more.

He stretched out on his back in the middle of the bed with his hands behind his head and his eyes closed. Myriad thoughts played through his mind. He tried to make a logical picture of the puzzle pieces he had gathered but didn't possess enough of them, at least not yet. He didn't want to make Cassie suspicious by asking questions that would seem to be none of his business. He also wanted to hear Bob Hampton's explanation of what he had intended to accomplish with the letter he sent to Randall.

About twelve thirty that afternoon, Trent headed for the harbor master's office to take care of his business there. Next, he wandered back to the restaurant to have lunch before it closed for the day. It hadn't been that long since he had breakfast. His primary intention was to check out the lunch business.

Cassie bustled back and forth between the counter and the tables, trying to keep up with everything. Trent slid quietly onto the only empty counter stool and watched the nonstop activity. She offered him a sincere if somewhat weary smile as she hurried past, carrying three plates of food. "I'll be right with you."

"Take care of your other customers first. I'm in no hurry."

Trent carefully scrutinized the routine of the restaurant. Cassie was shorthanded and trying to do it all—wait on customers, handle drink orders from the bar, and be the cashier. She obviously needed help. The restaurant would be closing in half an hour. He wanted to get a feel for the restaurant and bar operation, and the best way to do that would be helping out during the rush.

He glanced into the bar area and saw a drink order on a tray waiting for Cassie to pick it up. He went into the bar, grabbed the tray, and carried it back into the restaurant without Mike noticing. He called to Cassie as she rushed past him. "Where do these go?"

Her look of surprise quickly disappeared as she offered him a grateful smile. "The beer goes to the end counter stool, the rest of them to the booth in the corner."

He quickly served the drinks, then returned the tray to the bar. Mike glared at him. "What do you think you're doin'? That tray's for the restaurant drinks."

"That's what I was doing, delivering the restaurant drinks." Without waiting for Mike's reaction, Trent left the bar and returned to his seat at the counter. Several people stood at the cash register waiting to pay their bill. The register was one of those old-fashioned types with individual keys for the money denominations and a *No Sale* key that opened the cash drawer rather than a computerized cash register. He went behind the counter and took control of the pay process.

Cassie hurried from the kitchen with her hands full. The sight of Trent at the cash register, taking in money and giving out change, grabbed her full attention. Shock immediately jolted her. A quick flash of anger surged through her body. What the hell did he think he was doing?

On closer scrutiny, her anger calmed a bit when she realized he had neatly stacked money with the accompanying lunch check next to the register and dispensed the proper change from the register drawer. At least he hadn't attempted to ring up the amounts using the wrong code keys, leaving her with a mess.

But still, she fully intended to let him know she didn't appreciate his arbitrary decision to take charge of her money.

She continued to bustle among tables, counter customers, the bar, and the kitchen while very mixed feelings bounced around inside her. He absolutely had no right to make himself at home with her money. If she hadn't been so swamped, she would have set him straight then and there. She kept a careful eye on him while continuing to take care of her customers. She expelled a quick sigh of resignation. At that point, she could only trust in his honesty and hope the cash drawer came close to balancing after she rang up all the lunch checks he had taken in then totaled the categories.

The last of the rush finally came to an end a few minutes after two o'clock, closing time for the restaurant. She locked the door, hung out the *Closed* sign, and turned her attention to the cash register.

She glared at him. "How dare you—"

He held up his hand to stop her from speaking. "I know. I had no business handling the money. But you were so rushed and had customers waiting. I decided it made more sense to try and appease you later than to have your customers unhappy because they had been kept waiting when they wanted to leave."

He offered her an apologetic smile. "As the always wise and ever-present *they* have said on numerous occasions, sometimes it's better to seek forgiveness than it is to ask permission."

"Yeah…well…" She had been fully prepared to land on him with both feet, but he had short-circuited her intentions by apologizing before she had a chance to say anything. Suddenly she felt a little bewildered and unsure about how to proceed. "You can tell the ubiquitous *they* that I am not amused."

Mustering as stern an attitude as she could, not an easy task considering the very unsettling impact his dazzling smile had on her, she voiced her displeasure. "Look, this is my restaurant. I own it and I run it. I have enough problems with Bob Hampton trying to ride rough shod over me and butting into my business. I don't appreciate strangers stepping in uninvited, taking over, and especially handling the money without my permission."

She continued before he could interrupt although her initial heated anger had cooled considerably. "I appreciate your intentions, but this is a small town with my clientele being mostly locals, especially when it's not tourist season. I won't lose customers just because I'm shorthanded today, and they had to wait a few minutes."

He reached out and clasped her hand in his as he looked at her for a long moment. "I was totally out of line in stepping in like that without your permission." His soft voice conveyed his sincerity. "I'm just not accustomed to small towns." He squeezed her hand. "Forgive me?"

Cassie slowly removed her hand from his electrifying touch. She needed to break the physical contact he initiated. As much as she did not want to admit it, his touch stirred desires in her. Desires that made her act impulsively in renting him the room. Desires that allowed her to dismiss his intrusion into her business with no more than a mild rebuke.

Desires that caused her insides to tremble.

"Okay, you're forgiven." She retained her stern

expression, wanting to make sure he understood how seriously she took the matter. "But this one time only. Don't let it happen again. Now, if you'll excuse me, I still have work to do."

"This time I'll ask. What do you need to do? Is there something I can help you with?" Trent's offer held an underlying ulterior motive. He wanted to see how much money the restaurant took in for breakfast and lunch. Things were busy at lunch, but when he had arrived mid-morning, there were no customers at all although she had alluded to a busy breakfast. Did this represent a typical business day?

"No, it's just the end-of-shift details." She began ringing up the checks Trent had taken in, adding the cash to the register drawer, then punching the total keys. "Ringing out the register, balancing the restaurant checks against the totals, taking care of the daily bank deposit, things like that. It doesn't take very long. It's when I have to deal with the actual bookkeeping that it takes longer."

She removed the cash drawer from the register and set it on the counter, then snapped the cover over the drawer. After gathering up the restaurant checks and setting them on the cash drawer, she reached underneath the counter, grabbed two ledgers, then added them to the top of the stack.

Trent thought back on the last half hour. He rather enjoyed the bustling activity and especially eavesdropping on the conversations between the customers. They had been open, friendly exchanges without the stress and pressure of needing to read between the lines to determine what someone really meant, to constantly second-guess someone's true motives. And no need to be ever vigilant of who might be listening in an attempt to gather information for their own purposes. As a Beverly Hills attorney with many high profile clients, he had to be on constant guard against that possibility whenever in public. He found it refreshing and surprisingly comfortable to be out of that atmosphere.

He picked up a newspaper someone had left on one of the counter stools.

Her voice quickly broke into his thoughts. "You're not going to throw that paper away, are you?"

"Well…yes, I was."

She took it from him. "Never throw newspapers away. I save them for the recycle stack at the corner market." She folded the paper neatly and stuck it under the counter with several other folded newspapers.

Cassie picked up the cash drawer and the items stacked on top of it. She struggled with the awkward configuration that looked as if it would topple over.

Trent moved quickly to her side. "Here, let me help you with that." He took the ledgers and restaurant checks, purposely leaving the cash drawer in her hands. "Where do you want this stuff?"

"Everything goes to my office." She held his gaze for a moment longer, then turned and left the restaurant through the back door with Trent following her.

They entered her house, and she climbed the stairs to the second floor. Trent's gaze remained glued to the fluid movements of her body as he continued to follow her. When they reached the top of the stairs, he saw her office straight ahead. He glanced quickly to the right, peering through an open door into her bedroom. He observed a bright, cheery room completely different from the rest of the house. It definitely did not look like something that belonged to a maiden aunt. It projected a feminine feel without being girly, the colors soft and muted. He observed the king-size bed and a dresser but didn't have a chance to see any more.

"Just put that on the table." She pointed, indicating the place.

"Is there anything I can help you with? I'm pretty handy with numbers and such." He leaned back against the table, his arms folded across his chest.

"No, thank you. This won't take me long." Cassie furrowed her brow into a slight frown. He may have taken it upon himself to handle the money at the register for a short period of time, but that didn't mean he needed to know how much money she took in for the day.

He tilted his head and raised a questioning eyebrow. "You're frowning. Is there anything wrong?"

A little tremor darted through her. She gave a fleeting thought to the excitement he caused in her on one hand and her wariness of him on the other. Or could her wariness be caused by her own unexpected desires? She shoved away the unwelcome intrusion. "No, it's just that it's been a hectic day. I was looking forward to a few minutes to relax with some peace and quiet."

He eyed her briefly, then extended a sexy smile. "After you finish your work here, how about coming back to the bar? I'll buy you a glass of wine."

"In the middle of the afternoon?"

"If it's okay to have a drink with lunch, then why wouldn't the middle of the afternoon be okay for a glass of wine?"

She cocked her head to one side and studied him for a moment, wondering how much personal involvement would be wise in a clearly business situation of him renting her room, then returned his smile. Desire won out over concern. "I'd enjoy that."

He gave her a quick wink as he headed toward her office door. "It's a date."

She watched as he left the office and descended the staircase. She heard the front door close. Cassie leaned back in her chair and closed her eyes. A mental image of Trent formed across the screen of her mind.

Trent Nichols—handsome and charming, a very disconcerting man. The way he made her feel inside disturbed her but not in a bad way. She had to admit she liked the sensation. It had been a long time since she felt that way. Even longer since she had been physically attracted to a desirable man. Her breathing increased slightly. She pictured his dazzling smile, his sparkling blue eyes...his sensuous mouth. What would a kiss from that mouth feel like? How would it taste?

She quickly opened her eyes and looked around. She shoved the totally inappropriate thoughts aside, took a steadying breath, then turned her attention to the work at hand.

****

Trent wandered into the bar and took a seat on the end bar stool. Mike's brusque attitude combined with the expression on his face clearly indicated his dislike for Trent. Ignoring Mike, he picked up a newspaper someone had left behind.

"Cassie saves those." Mike immediately snatched the paper away from him and folded it.

"Yes, I know. She told me she saves them for the

recycling bin at the market." He gestured toward the newspaper. "I was going to look at it, not throw it away."

Trent maintained a neutral attitude. Mike didn't return the paper to him, an obvious effort to establish his authority over the happenings in the bar similar to an animal marking its territory.

"You here for some reason?" Mike's curt tone and clipped words clearly conveyed his feelings. "This is a bar. If you don't want somethin' to drink, then move on."

Trent looked around, noting that most of the afternoon customers were drinking beer, then returned his attention to Mike. He started to ask what red wines they served by the glass, then decided against it. A small bar like this one probably served only one red, one white, and one blush by the glass. "I'll have a glass of red wine."

Mike muttered under his breath as he turned to get the drink. "Humph, it figures. *Wine*."

Trent interpreted Mike's attitude as a basic skepticism about everything, not just Trent's presence. Many years of a highly successful law practice with more court trials than he could count had taught him how to quickly size up people and accurately read them.

He took a sip of wine, pleasantly surprised to find it a much better quality than he had anticipated. Something else he had learned from his years as a top rated attorney—in addition to being careful of what he said in public, there was also the need to keep his ears open and take in what other people said. The local gossip turned out to be full of interesting little tidbits about the town and its people. He heard Bob Hampton's name mentioned on several occasions and never in a favorable way. He sat quietly sipping his wine and listening to the conversation. As with the lunch crowd in the restaurant, everyone seemed open and the life style straight-forward and uncomplicated.

Then a bit of conversation floated across the room that grabbed his full attention. Someone at a table behind him mentioned the newly arrived sixty-foot yacht docked at the harbor. The Marina Del Rey, California, designation on the stern was the source of curiosity. It was a long way from its home base. He tried to tune in on the conversation, to catch everything being said, but a cacophony of distracting noise prevented it. He casually swiveled around on the stool as if looking around the bar, his true intention to see who was talking.

"Hi." Cassie's voice interrupted his concentration.

"Hi, yourself. Shall we sit at a table?" He picked up his glass of wine and turned to Mike. "A glass of white wine, please." As he rose to escort Cassie to an empty table in the corner, Trent caught Mike's look of disapproval.

As soon as they were seated, she immediately commented on his proprietary manner, her voice teasing yet still conveying a hint of irritation. "You did it again."

He looked at her in surprise. "Did what?"

"Made decisions for me without consulting me first. I don't recall saying I wanted a glass of white wine. Maybe I don't like white wine."

"You look like a white wine type of person to me. And I saw a couple of bottles of white wine in your kitchen. Is there something you'd rather have?"

"No…it's just that I would have preferred you asking me first."

He caught the hint of irritation and matched it to the way she had taken him to task less than an hour ago. "I'm sorry. It's a bad habit of mine. If I get out of line again, feel free to give me a swift kick in the seat of the pants." He offered a sincere smile and extended his hand toward her. "Forgive me…again?"

She returned his smile as she accepted his handshake. "Yes, I forgive you…*again*." Her expression changed from a smile to something more stern. "But this is definitely the last time."

He took a sip of his wine as Mike set a glass in front of Cassie, shot Trent a sideways glare, and returned to the bar. Trent engaged Cassie in conversation, hoping to elicit some information about her business operation. "That was a pretty good rush of business at lunch, especially with it being later than the traditional noon to one o'clock lunch hour, and it looks like there're quite a few customers in here right now. Is this normal for midafternoon on a weekday? Are things always this busy?"

"It gets busier as we move into the summer season. Being right next to the ferry landing has its blessings and its curses. Once people have their cars in line, they end up in here while waiting for the ferry arrival and time to load. That gives us a lot of extra business, but also some pretty hectic moments. I always need additional help during the summer tourist season."

A slight grin turned the corners of her mouth. "I originally thought you were out of money and looking for work. After you mentioned the motel, I assumed you must have gone there looking for a summer job. In fact, I was going to offer you a job until you insisted on paying for your breakfast and paid in advance for renting my spare room. That told me you weren't homeless or down on your luck and in immediate need of work." The crimson flush of embarrassment came to her cheeks as she lowered her gaze.

Once again she had said something that caught him totally by surprise. The idea that she had planned to offer him a job for no more reason than her assumption that he was down on his luck presented a totally unexpected turn of events. She knew nothing about him. He could have been an escaped criminal on the run, looking for a place to hide. Cassie Brockton was certainly a very special lady.

He reached out and lightly touched her cheek. He allowed his fingertips to linger for a moment as he captured eye contact with her. "That's very gracious of you. It's not often one finds someone who's willing to go out of their way for a stranger."

She quickly lowered her gaze as the blush on her cheeks turned a deeper shade of red. "Please, you're embarrassing me."

She appeared to have let down her guard a little, but she had brought up the subject of the motel. It gave him his opening to ask about it. "Speaking of the motel…you seem to be having problems with the motel owner. You mentioned something earlier about him continually butting into your business?"

A quick look of anger again flashed across her face. "Bob Hampton!"

There it was again, her antagonism toward Bob Hampton. He took a chance on a casual question, hoping it would not further anger her. "Why would you have problems with this guy? This is your business. What makes him think he has any say so about how you run things?"

Cassie eyed him carefully, as if turning his question over in her mind while deciding how to respond. A certain wariness showed on her face. "You seem to have quite a bit of interest in the motel. Do you know Bob Hampton?" She paused a moment before continuing. "Are you a business associate of his?"

Trent gave her a straight forward answer without hesitation. "I've never met him, never talked to him, wouldn't know him if he walked through the door. The motel seems to be a source of irritation for you. I find it odd that, with such a prime location, it isn't open for business with the tourist season approaching or at least showing some signs of preparing to open for the summer. I found it curious, that's all."

"I own this building and the businesses operating inside it, I own the house I live in, but Bob Hampton owns the land. Twenty-five years ago, my Aunt Sofie signed a ninety-nine year lease with Bob's mother for this half of the land."

So that was it. Bob owned all the land and the motel, but a long-term lease on the land stood in his way. Bob Hampton was trying to pull something, probably trying to sell off everything including the structures she owned without her knowing about it, and at the same time swindling a prospective buyer by not disclosing the information about the lease. He needed to get his hands on that lease and find out how things stood legally and what provisions there might have been to cover the current situation where neither of the two original parties to the lease were still alive.

Chapter Three

"That makes sense. I'm glad I turned him down." Randall's voice conveyed his relief.

"It could really be a nice little operation if handled properly. I've rented a room from Cassie Brockton. That puts me in a pretty good position to observe what's going on. I might want to go through you to make Bob Hampton some kind of an offer. I'll keep in touch and let you know when he shows up from wherever he's been." Trent terminated the call.

He made several notations in his computer file, then reflected on the two hours he and Cassie had spent together that afternoon.

Articulate, witty, charming, and comfortable to be around without being full of pretense. She also had a spirited independence he admired, even if they had crossed swords more than once during their brief acquaintance. It still surprised him, the way she had berated him for taking the initiative to help out at lunch. He had assumed she would be grateful for the assistance rather than angry.

He wrinkled his brow in a moment of reflection. He had been told more than once that he didn't always take the other person into consideration when intently digging to get to the bottom of something, when searching for the truth during a court case. His clients were high profile people, but his goal was not to protect the guilty just because they were rich and famous.

He didn't like hearing about his shortcomings. Could he be acting too aggressively in this matter, especially considering the circumstances? It's not as if it had been a court case he needed to win. The last thing he wanted to do was stomp on Cassie's realm.

He clicked on television and watched the news but couldn't get interested in any of the evening programs. His thoughts turned to Cassie, wondering what she was doing. A restlessness gripped him. He finally snapped off the television and left his room.

Trent wandered over to the motel and walked completely around it, looking in windows wherever possible and generally giving it closer scrutiny than his original inspection. It would need a lot of work, but he could clearly visualize the results. The more he contemplated the possibilities, the more he warmed to the idea. He left the motel and walked along the sidewalk in front of the restaurant, heading toward the waterfront.

"Trent."

He looked up at the sound of his name. "Cassie…" How long had she been standing there? Had she been watching him as he checked out the motel? "I didn't see you there." He walked up the pathway to the bar, indicating the door. "Are you coming or going?"

"I was just leaving. I always check in with Mike about this time to see if he needs help." She hesitated for a moment, then continued. "Did I see you coming from the motel? It's still closed, isn't it?"

"I was just looking it over. A bit of curiosity following our conversation. Since it's very close to summer season, I was looking to see if there were any signs of someone preparing to open the motel for business."

"It used to be open year round. I'm not sure what Bob Hampton's up to or where he's gone." She eyed him warily. "You seem a lot more interested than just idle curiosity."

He offered her a dazzling smile. "I was about to take a walk along the waterfront, look around a bit. Could I persuade you to join me? Possibly act as tour guide?"

Cassie noted the way he had abruptly changed the subject, as if he didn't want to continue with her train of thought or where it might lead. "No, I have some work to do in my office. Maybe some other time."

"Okay. I'll see you later." He stuck his hands into his pockets and casually strolled across the street.

Trent didn't return to Cassie's house until late that evening, letting himself into his room through the private entrance. It had been a long day, and he was tired. He had noticed the lights shining through the curtains of the second floor windows. She was still awake.

He had just pulled off his shirt when he heard a knock at his door followed by a click as she released the bolt lock on her side.

Cassie's jeans and crisp blouse were gone, and in their place, she wore a long velour robe in a rich peacock blue with white lace at the neck and the cuffs of the long sleeves. She stood there, barefooted with her toenails painted a pale coral shade that matched the color dotted on her soft lips. She looked enticingly sexy, despite the fact that the robe covered her from neck to toes.

Her slightly damp hair smelled of a light rose scent, a sweet but clean fragrance. She had obviously just gotten out of the bathtub and had prepared to go to bed. He felt a slight rush as he gazed into her green eyes. There was something so real about her, so honest. He fought an overwhelming desire to sweep her into his arms and kiss her very tempting mouth but managed to keep his errant desires in check, albeit with great difficulty.

He stood in front of Cassie, dressed in jeans and holding his shirt in his hand, his chest as tanned as his face and arms, his body taught and athletic without being muscle-bound. It took all her willpower to keep from reaching out and touching the sandy-colored hair that curled across his hard chest in perfect symmetry.

She tried to concentrate, but her mind kept wandering back to their conversations about Bob Hampton and Trent's curious behavior of inspecting the motel. He was definitely being very secretive about something. Signals of caution raced through her body and lodged in her mind.

The way his clear blue eyes looked her over, then settled on her eyes made her insides jump—again. This very unsettling feeling came over her every time they were together. A sensation that shoved her other concerns about him from her mind. "I, uh, knocked on your door an hour ago. I guess you were out."

"I just got back from my walk." His voice softened, his manner became reflective, and a faraway look settled in his eyes. "I've been trying to sort out some things in my mind, determine some priorities."

Cassie nervously ran her fingers through her blonde hair. "I, uh, just wanted to see if you needed anything before I turned in for the night. Do you have enough towels?" The butterflies flitted around inside her stomach as she looked into his steady gaze. Without touching her, he managed to draw her to him like a moth to a flame. Their close proximity produced shivers of excitement as her breathing increased.

Their combined desires permeated the air, an unmistakable electricity that neither could deny even if they wanted to.

Touching him, feeling his lips on hers, tasting his kiss—the concept a totally preposterous one. She knew nothing about him, not even where he came from. She had already exhibited truly questionable judgment by renting him a room. But something about him made her throw caution to the wind, something that made her feel adventurous and free spirited, something that made her want to explore all the possibilities, and indulge the feelings he stirred in her.

Trent, too, experienced very similar sensations that created an awkward situation for him. Living under Cassie's roof while evaluating the possibility of taking over the motel operation as a personal investment. Ownership of the land would be an investment that could infringe on her livelihood. It was beginning to seem more questionable than he originally thought. Perhaps poor judgment on his part to establish a personal relationship with one of the involved parties? An idea he didn't want to pursue.

Besides, when he first encountered Cassie, he had no idea of her connection to Bob Hampton. But that rationalization did nothing to ease his concerns.

Cautiously reaching his hand toward her face, he lightly touched the silky smoothness of her cheek, then quickly withdrew. The words popped into his head, as bold and loud as if he had actually spoken them for all to hear. *Oh, what a tangled web we weave...*

He wanted to stop the deception right now, tell her the truth before it grew to such proportions that it became thoroughly entrenched, driving an invisible wedge between them that couldn't be removed, a chasm too wide to span. He wanted to, but he couldn't. He still had his commitment to Randall to provide him with information about Bob Hampton and exactly what he wanted to sell...assuming that had even been Hampton's intention in contacting Randall.

Trent yearned to know everything about Cassie. Most certainly intellectually and emotionally. And also intimately. If he revealed his identity, what he did for a living, and why he had stopped at the island, he would be put in a position where he would be forced to leave, especially in light of her expressed intense dislike of attorneys. He felt sure she would immediately order him out of her house.

Cassie shivered with anticipation. Her curiosity and desires could no longer be held in. She had not been able to resist the overwhelming temptation any longer. She reached her face up to his and brushed a tentative kiss against his lips. After a moment's hesitation on his part, a fleeting hint of surprise combined with uncertainty that darted across his face, Trent returned her kiss. She found his mouth to be every bit as sensual as she had imagined, his kiss filled with excitement. She resisted the temptation to put her arms around him, the only physical contact between them being their lips. As if following her lead, he didn't enfold her in his embrace or touch her in any way other than the kiss.

After a lingering moment, she pulled back from his face and looked into his eyes. The sky-blue color had darkened into a smoldering blue intensity. The room crackled with electrical energy. Her words were tinged with just a hint of huskiness and an embarrassed hesitation. "I, uh…" She allowed her gaze to drop to the floor for a moment before recapturing eye contact with him. "I've been wondering what kissing you would be like ever since I fell off that ladder and into your arms. I don't need to speculate any longer. Now the curiosity is satisfied and the temptation put to rest."

She stepped back and closed his bedroom door, then hurried upstairs.

Trent finished undressing and went to bed, but sleep eluded him. He stared up at the ceiling, unable to force his eyes closed. He had never had that happen to him in just that way—so straight forward and honest, no silly games or pretenses. They had each felt the pull, each curious about exploring that magnetism. While he had fought temptation, she had taken the initiative and been the aggressor. As she said, now the curiosity had been satisfied and daily life could move forward without the nagging curiosity hanging in the air.

Yep…those had been her words, the sentiment she conveyed. The only problem being that nothing had been put to rest, at least not from his point of view. From the moment her lips brushed lightly against his, even before they came to rest on his mouth, he knew he wanted much more. Her taste proved to be every bit as sweet as he thought it would be, every bit as exciting. It took all his will power to keep from pulling her into his arms and thrusting his tongue between her lips. His will power and the fact that she had pulled away before he could act on those desires.

Nothing had been resolved. For him, the quick kiss had increased his desires many times over. Now, more than ever, he wanted to know everything about her—what made her laugh, what made her cry, her hopes, her dreams. And at the same time he wanted to intimately know all of her—her needs, her desires, what excited her, how to please her, the sensation of her touch against his body…of falling asleep with her in his arms and waking up with her still there.

Could she be having as much difficulty falling asleep as he was? A little tremor darted through his body. What had he gotten himself into? Would he ever be able to straighten out the mess he had created and reveal the truth? What was he doing? True, she represented a breath of fresh air in his life, but he had just met her. She was certainly not the only woman in the world.

He shoved the disturbing thoughts aside and turned his mind from personal to the business at hand. He tried to estimate the dollar amount taken in at the restaurant and the bar. Had it been a typical business day? He needed to get a look at her books.

He closed his eyes, desperately seeking out the release of sleep.

****

Upstairs in her bed, Cassie tossed and turned in an attempt to get to sleep. Could Trent be experiencing the same type of difficulty? The feel of his lips against hers remained emblazoned on her mind. The initial curiosity had, indeed, been satisfied, but it left an even greater temptation, now stronger than ever. There had been an awkward moment when she thought Trent was about to embrace her. When she had stepped back to avoid his arms, she saw the surprise and confusion on his face. Neither of them had said anything as they looked into each other's eyes for a long moment.

She had turned away first. Her voice had been soft and filled with the emotion of the moment as she tried to put things back on a more impersonal level. She had spoken the words in an attempt to stop the moment before it had moved beyond her control. "Good night, Trent. I'll see you in the morning."

"Good night, Cassie."

She had heard the same longing in his voice that coursed through her veins.

One thought had continued to run through her mind as she had climbed the stairs to her bedroom. Who was Trent Nichols, and why was he on her island?

****

"Mike tells me you've rented out your spare room to some stranger who wandered in yesterday morning. That was a pretty impulsive decision, wasn't it?" A note of caution invaded Jake's voice as he sipped his coffee.

"Mike worries too much." She tried to project a casual manner, treating the situation in a light vein. "Trent is very nice, and for reasons unknown, Bob seems to have the motel closed. I can use the extra money. It's no different than when Aunt Sofie rented the room out to strangers."

"It's not safe. You're a woman living alone—"

"So was Aunt Sofie. The inside door to the room bolt locks from inside my house. He only has access to his room from the porch without being able to go into the rest of the house or needing to enter or exit through it. His key only unlocks the door from the porch to his room. It doesn't unlock the door to my house." The thought suddenly hit her that she had not bothered to bolt the door last night when she had gone upstairs to her bedroom.

"Where is he? I'd like to meet this stranger who has apparently managed to turn your normally sensible head."

Cassie laughed as she poured more coffee into Jake's mug, then glanced at the clock on the wall. "Stop letting Mike influence you before you've even met Trent. He'll probably be in for breakfast. You can inspect him then."

"I'm not trying to pry into your business, but, uh, it's just that Mike doesn't seem to care for the guy very much. Thinks he's hiding something. I think you should be cautious, that's all. I don't trust Bob Hampton. This guy could be someone Bob sent here to undermine your operation. You know your lease is the only thing that's kept him from selling everything. He hasn't figured out how to get around it…yet."

Trent's voice interrupted their conversation as he entered the restaurant. "Good morning, Cassie."

"Good morning." She smiled at him. Their gazes locked for a brief moment before she turned her head toward Jake. "Trent, this is Jake Dorsey. Jake, this is Trent Nichols. He's rented my spare room for the duration of his visit on the island."

The two men shook hands.

"Nice to meet you, Jake." Trent seated himself on the next stool and took a sip of the coffee Cassie had placed in front of him.

Jake carefully engaged Trent in seemingly casual conversation. "So, Trent, what brings you to our island?"

"Nothing in particular. I've been doing some traveling and found myself here in my journey. It felt like a comfortable place to spend some time."

"That sounds interesting, just taking some time to see the country. I imagine you've seen some interesting things. As for me, I've spent most of my life right here."

"From the little I've seen, this seems like a nice place to live."

"What type of work do you do that allows you the availability of being able to travel around for an extended period of time? Are you perhaps a teacher at a location where the school term is over for the summer?"

"No, not a school teacher, but I have taught a couple of classes over the years."

"Where do you come from?"

"I've lived in several places." Trent took another sip of his coffee.

A little frown wrinkled across Jake's forehead.

Cassie kept glancing at the clock. Shortly before eleven o'clock, Jake and Trent were the only customers in the restaurant where they had been carrying on a conversation all morning. Mike was late, not like him at all. Cassie went into the bar to begin setting it up for lunch.

About ten minutes later, Mike came in the door. It only took one quick glance—red watery eyes, skin dry and pale. He had no business being at work.

"Sorry I'm late, I…" Mike's raspy voice could not get any more words out.

She immediately rushed to his side and put her

hand on his forehead. "You're running a temperature. What are you doing here? You should be home in bed. Now turn around and get out of here. Go home."

Mike carefully eyed Trent sitting at the counter and obviously listening to their conversation. "With Charlene gone, it would leave you impossibly shorthanded. I can get through the day okay."

"No way. We just won't open the bar until the restaurant closes at two o'clock. That way I'll only have to do drinks for the restaurant customers. If you refuse to consider your own health, then think about my customers." She gave him a teasing grin. "How can they come here and spend their money if you give all of them the flu and they have to stay home sick? I don't even want to think about what the health department would say. Now—" She physically turned him toward the door. "—go home."

Mike again tossed a very suspicious look in Trent's direction, then turned back toward her. "Are you sure you can manage?"

"I'm positive. Now get out of here. If you need anything, give me a call." She watched as Mike reluctantly made his way back out the door and walked down the street to his small house a couple of blocks away.

Cassie turned toward Jake with a questioning look. "What's on your schedule for today? Do you think you could help me in the bar until I close the restaurant?"

Disappointment crossed his face. "I'm sorry, Cassie. I've got a fishing charter to take out in half an hour. Otherwise, you know I'd do it."

Trent had obviously been carefully following the conversation. "I'd be happy to help you. I don't have anything special planned for the day."

She eyed him carefully. "Do you know how to tend bar?"

"As long as no one orders one of those obscure drinks with half a dozen ingredients that's made in the blender and topped off with a basket of fruit and one of those little paper umbrellas."

She laughed an open, easy laugh. "Not around here. An occasional martini, but nothing more difficult than that. It's mostly beer, wine, and your basic well drinks." She looked up into his eyes, the smile fading from her face. "Are you sure you don't mind? I don't expect you to do it for free. I'll pay you for a bar shift." Their gazes locked again as a sensual electricity danced between them.

"That won't be necessary. I'm happy to be able to help out"—he flashed a dazzling smile—"especially since I'll have your permission. This time you won't have any excuse for being mad at me...again."

Heat flushed across her cheeks as she lowered her eyelids.

Jake rose from the counter seat, took the last swallow of his coffee, and headed for the door. He shot a questioning look in Trent's direction, then addressed his comments to Cassie. "I'll check in with you as soon as I get back."

"Okay, Jake." She turned her attention to Trent. "Come on, I'll show you where everything is and how it functions."

Before they could get to the bar, the restaurant door opened and a man entered. She had never seen him before. He walked to the cash register and stood there, not taking a seat as a customer would. She hurried behind the counter and quickly looked him over. He wore an ill-fitting wrinkled suit with frayed cuffs on both the pants and jacket and scuffed shoes in desperate need of a shine.

He looked her up and down, then spoke. His voice carried just a hint of superiority. "Is the boss man in?"

"May I help you?" Her muscles tensed slightly at his tone, and her jaw tightened almost imperceptibly.

"No, girlie. I need to speak to the man in charge."

Cassie stared at the stranger, looking him right in the eye. "I'm the *person* in charge. What is it you want?"

"No, girlie." His voice clearly showed his irritation at her apparent inability to understand what he wanted. "I want to talk to the man who owns this place."

Cassie took a calming breath to steady her mounting anger. "My name is not *girlie,* and *I* own this establishment. Now, what is it you want?"

He immediately attempted to correct his mistake. He smiled, removed a business card from his jacket pocket, and handed it to her. "Name's Hemple. Couldn't help noticing your building here needs some repair work. Roof looks like it has some bad spots, sides need painting, rain gutters need repairing—"

"Mr. Hemple—" Trent's voice broke into the conversation. "Do you have a contractor's license? We couldn't possibly consider availing ourselves of your services without having your license number and checking it out with the state agency that issued it. We'd also need a list of references, people you've provided contracting services for in the last few months, specifically customers here on the island."

Cassie looked at Trent. A combination of mounting

anger and curiosity welled inside her. He had asked precise questions, his voice controlled, his words clipped, and his intimidating manner making it clear that he was in charge. She allowed a slight frown. For a moment, he had sounded like an attorney at a trial cross-examining a witness.

"Look here, fella." Hemple turned his attention to Trent, obviously not knowing quite what to make of the situation. "The girlie and I was havin' a business conversation."

Trent leveled a steady look at Mr. Hemple, his stare so intense that it looked as if it could bore into the man's very soul. He gestured toward Cassie. "This is a *lady*, not—"

"The *girlie* and you have concluded this conversation, Mr. Hemple." Cassie's voice took control of the situation before the exchange of words got out of hand. "Your services are not wanted. Goodbye." She glared at the man. He looked back at her, glanced at Trent, then left the restaurant.

She turned her attention to Trent who immediately dropped his gaze to the floor as he awkwardly shifted his weight from one foot to the other. "That was quite a little speech. Once again, *Mr. Nichols*, you seem to have appointed yourself the person in charge of *my* business dealings." Cassie's voice clearly conveyed her resentment at this most recent intrusion. And she hadn't finished letting him know.

"You sounded like you knew exactly what you were talking about, like you had participated in similar conversations at other times." She allowed a frown to furrow her brow as her jaw tightened. "You sounded just like..." She paused, then spat out the words as if they were poison "…just like some damn *attorney*."

Trent inwardly flinched at her tone. She again made her contempt and disgust for anything associated with an attorney blatantly obvious. He knew he had been wrong to interfere, knew he would probably incur her wrath, but he couldn't stop himself. He felt an overwhelming need to protect her. From the moment she had fallen into his arms, he had felt a sense of responsibility for her safety and well-being.

He looked up and smiled, trying to recover from his impulsive blunder. He didn't like the angry sparks flashing from her eyes. "Comes from watching too much television, especially police and lawyer shows. I just gave him my best *Law & Order* courtroom impression with a little bit of *Perry Mason* thrown in for good measure. He extended the pleading look of a little boy who had been caught with his hand in the cookie jar…*again*…and knew he would be punished. "I'm sorry. It was just that he was so obviously a crook and a con man trying to rip you off—"

"And you decided I wasn't smart enough to figure that out for myself?" Her tone remained angry.

He slowly shook his head. "That's not it at all."

"Then what?"

"Well…I guess when I caught you as you fell from the ladder that sort of made me responsible for you—for your well-being."

"That's ridiculous!" She stood with her hands on her hips, glaring at him.

Trent reached out and touched her cheek. "I find you very intelligent." He searched the depths of her green eyes as he cupped her face in his hands and lowered his head to hers. "And very desirable."

Chapter Four

Before Cassie could stop him, she felt Trent's mouth on hers and the heat of his kiss. All her anger disappeared in a puff of smoke, one that bordered on being an incendiary ball of fire. The kiss lasted only a few seconds, but it scorched right through to her soul. Putting up even the slightest resistance was not a consideration.

"Once again, I'm sorry for interfering with your business." His voice soft, his fingers lightly traced the outline of her lips. "I seem to always be apologizing to you."

She tried to regain control, not only of her emotions but also the situation. She stepped away from his mesmerizing presence, nervously ran her fingers through her hair, and took a calming breath. "It's...it's because you keep doing things that require an apology."

A teasing grin turned the corners of his mouth. "I guess it's just my naturally pushy nature."

"Well, maybe that works wherever you come from, but it doesn't work around here." She turned and headed toward the bar. The heated moment had passed. "There's work to do, and it's almost lunchtime."

Trent followed her.

Cassie made no mention of his kiss, gave no indication of how it had affected her. She went through the cash register procedures with him, showed him where things were stored, and filled him in on the regular customers he would probably encounter. After that, she returned to the restaurant to prepare for the lunch crowd.

"It's been quite a morning so far." Berta spoke up from the door to the kitchen.

Cassie glanced toward the bar, then returned her attention to Berta. "It hasn't been dull, that's for sure."

"Do you want me to call my niece to help with lunch? She could be here in fifteen minutes."

"I think we'll probably be able to make it okay. So far today hasn't been the rush we had yesterday. I'm sure we'll be fine."

Fortunately, Cassie's words were true. Lunch didn't turn into the hassled rush of yesterday. She bustled from table to counter but managed to keep up with the customers. In addition to the drink orders coming from the restaurant, Trent had several bar customers. He managed to handle it all without too many problems.

Finally, two o'clock arrived. Cassie put out the *Closed* sign, locked the restaurant entrance, then went into the bar. "How's it going?"

Trent offered a weary smile. "It's been a little hectic, but everything's okay. Now that I've gotten the hang of the routine, this evening should be much easier for me."

"What do you mean *this evening*?"

"You can't work from five o'clock this morning until late tonight, then again at five o'clock tomorrow morning. You'll end up collapsing from exhaustion, maybe even making yourself sick."

"Look—"

His stern expression did as much to cut off her words as his voice did. "No, *you* look. I'm right and you know it. Now, there's no reason why I can't finish out the day here. You go and take care of your restaurant business, and I'll take care of the bar customers." He stood his ground, not backing down from her angry glare.

Cassie started to say something, started to vent her anger over his totally unacceptable behavior, but she stopped herself. In spite of his pushiness, she conceded that what he said made sense. She let out a sigh as her anger subsided. "I'm going to tend to the restaurant close out, then I have some personal business to handle. We'll discuss tonight's work schedule later."

She took the cash drawer from the restaurant and went to her office. She quickly dispensed with her bookkeeping chores, prepared her bank deposit, and checked her list of errands, then leaned back in the chair and closed her eyes.

Her thoughts gravitated to Trent Nichols and the excitement his nearness stirred in her. No matter how angry he made her, it seemed that all he needed to do was touch her cheek and her anger dissolved. She pressed her fingertips to her lips, recalling the kiss they had shared earlier, the heat of his barely concealed passion.

After the turmoil of her marriage, her life was finally running in a smooth and orderly fashion. She liked living on the island, did not miss the big city hassle of Chicago, or the stress and pressure of her banking career. Things were so straight forward and honest here. Everyone and everything exactly who and what they appeared to be.

Then one morning, this stranger showed up from out of nowhere and...

Cassie refused to finish the thought. She took care of her errands and did not return to the bar until almost six o'clock that evening. She found things much busier than she thought they would be. Trent was swamped as he tried to fix drinks and wait on tables all at the same time. She immediately took over the tables and caught him up on washing the dirty glasses.

She made a mental note to have a dishwasher installed in the bar. Mike had mentioned it when she had installed one in the kitchen, but she had not realized the necessity until she saw the backlog of dirty glasses. Since Trent was alone and unaccustomed to working in a bar, he had not been able to wash glasses while handling drinks and waiting on tables. Business stayed brisk for the rest of the evening.

Cassie continued to help Trent until they finally closed at eleven thirty. After locking the bar door behind the last customer, she plopped down on a bar stool and breathed a sigh of relief. "Wow! That was quite a rush. There's probably some sort of corollary between being short-handed and having a sudden increase in business."

"I'll buy you a drink." He reached for a wine glass, then stopped and turned to her. "What would you like?"

She looked at him for a minute, then managed a weary smile. "Well, at least you asked this time. However, I'm so tired that a drink would probably put me to sleep before I can get to bed." Their gazes locked together. Her pulse rate increased.

Trent poured her a glass of wine in spite of her less than positive response, set it in front of her, then poured one for himself. He took a sip as he watched her stifle a yawn.

"You must be beyond exhaustion." His soft voice was almost a caress as he reached out and lightly touched her cheek. Then he dropped his hand to the bar, resting it next to hers. "Would you like me to help you in the restaurant in the morning? I could open if you'd like. It would give you an extra couple of hours sleep."

"I can't do that. It's my responsibility to open the restaurant." She was more than aware of his touch as he slowly laced their fingers together. With her other hand, she lifted her glass to her lips and sipped the wine.

Trent, too, took a sip of his wine. Their eyes met across the rims of the glasses. She lowered the glass from her mouth. He set his glass on the bar and leaned his face forward until their lips brushed. Then he brought his mouth fully against hers.

Cassie was not sure what to do, how to respond. He excited her senses as no one ever had, causing very disconcerting emotions to well inside her. She didn't want Trent to get the wrong idea, to think she was some sort of love-starved woman living alone on an island, one who would easily fall prey to his charms. Or, worse yet, that she could be easily swayed by every good-looking stranger who crossed her path.

She allowed herself to briefly return his kiss before pulling away. Her words came out barely above a whisper. "It's late, and I need to be up very early."

"You're right." He again leaned his face into hers and captured her mouth with a kiss. Though soft, it spoke emotional volumes about the sensuality of the man.

She experienced a shortness of breath and

palpitations of her heart as the intensity of the kiss deepened. She wanted—no, make that *needed*—to explore the sensations he created in her. In the dimness of the bar, Cassie seated on a stool leaning across it and Trent standing behind the bar leaning forward, she returned the barely hidden passion of his kiss. In the distance, a ship's horn could be heard. No other sounds existed beyond their breathing.

Trent felt the heat of Cassie's energy as she returned his kiss. Her taste was intoxicating, almost addictive, as he cautiously darted his tongue into the tenderness of her mouth. She did not pull away from him. With their fingers still entwined, he took his free hand and caressed the softness of her cheek.

He felt torn between two dynamics. On one hand, there was his rapidly building desire for her and on the other hand his discomfort about his deception combined with the tentative plans he had formulated in the back of his mind. He knew who he was and he knew who she was, but she didn't have a clue to his true identity, where he came from, or what he really wanted. She accepted him at face value and trusted him on blind faith. That type of instant trust was not part of the day-to-day reality of the world where he lived and made his fortune. The possible consequences of his deception weighed heavily on his conscience.

She drew her mouth slightly away from his, leaving just the barest touch of contact lingering between their lips. "This...this isn't a good idea." Her words came out as a mere whisper. She visibly tried to recover her composure and put more authority into her voice. "It's very late, and I'm tired."

Trent's lips brushed against hers for just a second

longer. Slowly, he released her hand from his grasp and stood up straight. "Yes...it's very late." He tried to keep the unsettling effect the kiss had on him from creeping into his voice—without much success. "But that doesn't mean this isn't a good idea."

He watched as Cassie efficiently went about the business of ringing out the register, removing the cash drawer, and setting it on the bar top. He turned out the lights except for the night light behind the bar, then he double checked the bolt lock on the front door. She took the cash drawer, and he picked up their half full wine glasses. They exited through the back door, Cassie making sure it was securely locked and the alarm set.

They walked up the path to the house. He waited as she unlocked the front door. "It's a nice night out. Why don't we sit on the swing and finish our wine?"

She regarded him and his request cautiously. "I don't know. It's awfully late."

He offered her a smile of encouragement. "Just until we finish our glass of wine?" He took the cash drawer from her and set it on the table inside the front door.

She moved toward the swing. "Okay, for a few minutes."

He sat next to her, and the swing gently swayed back and forth. "I can see why you like living here. It's very comfortable, very real..." He stopped talking, afraid he might have said too much.

She immediately picked up on his words and his hesitation. "*Very real*. That's an odd thing to say." She turned her face toward him, her features highlighted by the light of the full moon. "Where do you come from, Trent? Where have you lived that wasn't real?"

"I was referring to the people as much as the place. Real people without pretenses. Even Mike. He doesn't like me, and he makes no effort to hide the fact. I much prefer that to someone who smiles at my face while twisting the knife in my back."

She swallowed the last sip of her wine and set the glass on the window ledge next to the swing. Again she faced him. "Who are you, Trent Nichols?" Her gaze held his. She seemed to be searching for some hidden truth.

"I'm...I don't know. I used to know, but I don't anymore. Somewhere along the way I seem to have lost myself to the vagaries of life."

Trent remained lost in his own thoughts for several minutes. He gradually became aware of her head resting on his shoulder. Her slow, even breathing told him she had fallen asleep. Moving slowly and carefully so he would not wake her, he gently lifted her in his arms, carried her inside the house, and up the stairs. He placed her on her bed, removed her shoes, and covered her with a blanket.

Trent hurried downstairs, locked the front door, and took the bar's cash drawer up to her office. He wasn't sure exactly what she did with the cash register tape, the bar checks, and the cash drawer. He decided to leave them on the table.

He paused at her bedroom door on the way to his room, then went back inside her bedroom. "Good night, Cassie." His words were uttered as a mere whisper, and his gaze lingered on her face a moment longer. He hesitated, then reached to the nightstand and shut off her alarm clock.

No question that he would catch hell from her in

the morning, but she needed the sleep.

****

"Trent!" Berta's obvious surprise showed on her face and in her voice when he appeared at four forty-five the next morning. She glanced toward the house as she unlocked the back door of the restaurant and turned off the alarm. "Is Cassie all right?"

"She opened up yesterday before five o'clock and closed up last night at almost midnight. She's getting some much needed sleep." Trent himself had gotten very little sleep, maybe three hours total. Even though he had been very tired when he climbed into bed, he had not been able to force himself to sleep. The kiss they had shared in the bar continued to play havoc with his senses. The feel of her snuggled in his arms as he carried her upstairs was still very real to him, as real as the memory of her cradled in his arms after her fall from the ladder.

Berta glanced at his empty hands. "You forgot the cash drawer. You'd better hurry back and get it. We open for business in fifteen minutes."

The cash drawer... He hadn't given it a thought. He knew where the drawer from the bar register was. He had put it on the table in Cassie's office. But the cash drawer from the restaurant? That presented a different problem. He quickly entered the house through his bedroom and went upstairs to the office, being very quiet so he didn't disturb her sleep. After five minutes of opening desk drawers and filing cabinet drawers, he finally found it on a shelf in the closet. He grabbed it and hurried back to the restaurant.

Even though he had watched Cassie go through the opening procedures for the bar, he was not sure exactly

66

how that related to the restaurant. So he busied himself doing what he thought were the most logical things— making coffee, setting out cream pitchers, and filling water glasses with ice. Jake was outside waiting as Trent removed the *Closed* sign and unlocked the front door at five o'clock.

Trent gave him a friendly smile. "Good morning, Jake. How are you today?"

"Good morning." Jake looked around, his manner reserved, his expression one of caution. "Where's Cassie?"

"She's exhausted. Hopefully she's getting some much needed sleep."

"I see." Jake stared out the window at the young man swaggering up the walkway toward the restaurant. "Damn! Here comes nothing but trouble."

Trent looked out the window, following Jake's gaze. "That guy walking this way? Who is he?"

"That's Bob Hampton. He owns the land under this restaurant and under Cassie's house. The kid's a real bad apple. He'll try to bully you into what he wants. Cassie stands up to him pretty good."

Trent allowed a slight frown as he clenched his jaw into a hard line. *So, the elusive Bob Hampton has finally made an appearance.*

Bob walked through the door and directly to the cash register as he looked around. "Where's Cassie?"

Trent made an immediate judgment concerning the arrogant young man standing on the other side of the counter. His tone, the expression on his face, his body language—everything about him grated on Trent's nerves. He was in his early twenties and wore the smug expression of someone who thought he knew it all, someone who believed in his own entitlement. Trent had seen it many times before on the faces of the spoiled adult children of his wealthy Beverly Hills clients—an arrogant attitude, a demeanor that thoroughly rankled him.

"She'll be in later. Is there something I can do for you?"

Bob Hampton looked Trent over, then dismissed him with a withering glance as someone inconsequential, not noticing the way Trent tightened his jaw and narrowed his eyes. "My business is with Cassie. Tell her to call me as soon as she gets here."

Trent maintained an expressionless mask, feigning ignorance of the situation. "Very well—can I have your name? Do you have a business card I can pass on to her?" He was pleased by Bob's adverse reaction to the realization that someone didn't know his identity.

His irritation at having to identify himself clearly evident, he spat out the angry words. "Tell her Bob Hampton wants to talk to her *immediately.*"

Trent grabbed a piece of paper and a pencil and made an elaborate show of jotting down the name. "That's Bob Hampton?" He looked up, taking pleasure in the irritation covering Bob's face. "And your phone number?"

"She knows where to find me." A hostile Bob Hampton turned and stormed out of the restaurant.

Without taking his eyes off Bob's retreating form, Trent crumpled the sheet of paper and tossed it in the waste basket beneath the counter.

If there had been any lingering doubts or concerns about the plans he had been formulating, they had just been resolved. Not only had this arrogant jackass been giving Cassie a bad time, he had now made an enemy of Trent Nichols. He would soon discover what a bad move that had been. One way or the other, he would see to it that Bob Hampton would no longer be a problem in Cassie's life.

The sounds of barely concealed chuckles reached his ears, bringing him out of his thoughts. He turned toward Jake who tried his best to suppress his laughter.

He looked at Trent with new admiration. "That was a good one. There's nothing that riles that little punk more than to have someone not know who he is."

Jake laughed out loud as he reached forward and extended his hand to Trent. The two men shook hands, the beginnings of a new friendship forming between them.

"I've been trying to get Cassie to take that lease agreement to a lawyer and have it looked over and thoroughly analyzed, but she refuses." Jake leaned forward and lowered his voice. "She used to be married to a lawyer and says she'd rather trust the devil than accept anything a lawyer says."

A little ripple of anxiety washed over Trent. But at least he now understood where her low opinion of attorneys originated—her ex-husband and what he had already learned was a contentious divorce.

The myriad thoughts that immediately consumed Trent were interrupted by the early morning regulars arriving for breakfast. He took Jake's order, poured him some coffee, then waited on the new arrivals as they seated themselves at the counter.

****

Cassie burst through the back door of the restaurant at nine thirty and descended on Trent, her words emphatic and angry. "How dare you do that to me!"

Trent looked around, feigning an expression of total innocence, as if trying to figure out where her words were directed. "Are you talking to me?"

"You know damn well I'm talking to you!" Her green eyes flashed fire. She quickly closed the distance between them, lowering her voice so the customers couldn't hear. "How dare you take over my business like this. At first, I thought I had turned off the alarm, forgotten about it, and fallen back asleep. Then I realized you must have turned it off when you apparently carried me upstairs."

He glared back at her. "You needed the sleep, and you know it, a fact proven by how late you slept. If you weren't so pigheaded, you'd admit it."

They locked horns, neither giving an inch.

"I'm pigheaded? Look who's talking! How many times have I told you to stay out of my business?"

"If you'd use a little more common sense, I wouldn't have to step in to protect you from yourself."

"And just who appointed you my protector?"

His manner instantly softened as he reached out and gently caressed her cheek. He knew she would be angry with him and had prepared for her reaction. "I appointed myself to that position the moment you fell off that ladder into my arms."

A pink flush covered her cheeks and embarrassment entered her eyes, replacing the anger.

"Actually, it's been a fairly quiet morning." He withdrew his hand, instantly consumed by the loss of the intimate touch. "Business has been steady, just enough to keep busy but not hectic. There was one thing." His brow wrinkled in thought. "Bob Hampton stopped by to see you. He said he wants you to call him...*immediately*."

Cassie's anger instantly flared again at the mention of the name. "That insufferable little jerk. I wonder what he wants now."

****

Jake sat on the end bar stool sipping his beer. "Did you and Trent get your little difference straightened out?"

Cassie frowned as she wiped off the bar. "Not exactly. We sort of let it drop for the time being." She picked up a discarded newspaper, folded it, and placed it beneath the counter with the others. Truth be known, the argument had ended the moment he reached out, touched her cheek, and looked into her eyes. Her insides had melted and her anger dissolved into a little puddle. The memory of his lips pressed against hers flooded through her reality. She had insisted he leave the restaurant, that she could handle the work load without his help.

"You would really have enjoyed the way Trent played Bob Hampton and how angry Bob was after his conversation with Trent."

"You seem to have raised your opinion of Trent. Now, if I could just get Mike to lighten up. He called a little while ago, says he'll be back to work tomorrow. I'm sure glad to hear that. Charlene gets back this afternoon. Now maybe things can return to normal."

"I'll have a little talk with Mike. I think he's off base about Trent. You can't help but like a guy who can get the best of Bob Hampton without even raising his voice let alone displaying any anger." Jake tilted his head to one side as a furrow wrinkled across his forehead. "There's a lot of intelligence and savvy there and a very commanding presence." He glanced at his watch. "Uh-oh. It's almost six o'clock. I've got to go."

"Where are you off to in such a rush?" Cassie gave him a teasing grin. "Big date tonight?"

Jake's cheeks turned a bright red as he glanced at the floor. "Well, I did ask Berta if she'd like to watch a movie with me. I bought some DVDs. One of them is a Fred Astaire and Ginger Rogers movie. Berta really likes their films."

Cassie reached across the bar and gave his cheek a little pat. "Why, you little devil, who would have guessed that you're really a closet romantic. Fred Astaire instead of John Wayne?"

He tried to appear irritated, an attempt that failed miserably. "Cut that out. It's just a movie with a friend."

She smiled knowingly. "Of course."

Chapter Five

When Cassie exited the back door after closing the bar for the night, she immediately spotted Trent sitting on the porch swing. He left the porch and joined her on the path. He had departed the restaurant that morning at her insistence, and she hadn't seen him for the rest of the day...until now.

"I'll carry that for you." He took hold of the cash drawer and the bar checks as they walked into the house. He set everything on the table in her office, then placed his hands on her shoulders. He seemed to be searching her face before settling his gaze on her eyes.

Her insides quivered. He had such a disconcerting effect on her. When he touched her, nothing in the world mattered except being with him. She didn't understand it nor did she like the helpless sensation, but that didn't mean it wasn't so.

"Will Mike be back tomorrow?" His tone emulated a verbal caress.

"Yes, he called this afternoon, said he was feeling much better, and would be in for sure. Charlene got back this afternoon." Cassie could barely force out the words. The pull of his magnetic spell drew her to him.

"Good." He laced their fingers together. "As soon as you close the restaurant tomorrow, let's go on a picnic. It's supposed to be a beautiful day, and I'd like to see more of the island. Besides, it would allow us to be away from the demands of your business." His voice took on a teasing quality. "Maybe we can spend some time together without anything causing an argument."

He totally mesmerized her, catching her in the ethereal net he had cast in her direction. "A picnic? But it would be going on three o'clock before we even got started. We couldn't do that."

"Why not? One of the nice things about being this far north is that it stays light well into the evening this time of year. It's still early May and look how late the daylight lingers." His tone seemed to almost challenge her. "Or do you have some sort of a rule about going on picnics with people who rent rooms from you?"

As she had done before with Trent, she threw caution to the wind. A picnic—being able to spend some leisurely time alone together. "Yes, going on a picnic sounds like a great idea." She would like that very much.

He pulled her into his arms and captured her mouth with a searing kiss, one that said far more than merely good night. Every physical encounter between them seemed to deepen her attraction to him. Somehow, he managed to muddle her thinking and sway her feelings with nothing more than a brushing of his lips against hers. The heat sizzled through her body as the kiss deepened, touching all of her. Breathing became more difficult, more labored. She finally broke the kiss. If it had continued, there was only one place it could lead.

She watched as Trent descended the stairs toward his room. She tried to still the tremors that coursed through her body as she went into her own bedroom and shut the door. Her fingertips touched her lips where his mouth had enveloped her in a good night kiss.

She thought back to other moments of closeness with Trent. Some of the things he had said, words that seemed to be more for himself than spoken to her. Words she found confusing such as his comment about living somewhere real, not understanding exactly what he meant. But she did know it meant a lot more than the surface words would indicate. It had come from deep inside him. Had he experienced such turmoil in his life that he had decided to simply drop out? Was that why he had wandered to the island? Seeking some type of sanctuary? A refuge of sorts?

She undressed and climbed into bed.

****

Cassie put the *Closed* sign in the restaurant window, then quickly tended to the end-of-shift details. It took twenty minutes. Now nothing stood between her and the picnic with Trent.

She collected one of the good bottles of wine from the bar, along with a couple of wine glasses, ignoring Mike's pointed glare of disapproval. She packed some baked chicken and a nice salad into a picnic basket.

Berta spoke hesitantly as if unsure about saying anything at all. "Uh, Cassie...don't you think maybe you're rushing things with Trent too much? You really don't know anything about him."

"It's just a picnic in the middle of the day. There's no reason to be uneasy." She dismissed Berta's concerns in the same way she had dismissed Jake's concerns and Mike's disapproval. Perhaps she was throwing caution to the wind, but she had made that choice. She simply could neither ignore nor quell the tremors of excitement Trent created in her.

Cassie drove them partway around the island,

stopping at a grassy bluff overlooking the channel. Trent spread the picnic blanket on the ground, and she set the picnic basket on the blanket.

"Come on." She grabbed his hand and gave it a tug as she headed toward the edge of the bluff. "Let's take a look." She released his hand and hurried ahead of him.

Trent caught up to her and reclaimed her hand, lacing their fingers together. "What are we looking for?"

"Whales. Killer whales—Orca. It's a little bit early, but we might get lucky. When the salmon invade these waters headed for their spawning grounds, the whales have a feast. It's their favorite food. It usually happens in June." She turned toward him. "Have you ever seen a killer whale in the wild? They're beautiful."

"In captivity, but not in the open ocean where they live. I've seen humpback whales on their annual migration along the west coast, but never the Orcas."

Trent released her hand, put his arm around her shoulders, and pulled her close to him. They stood in silence for fifteen minutes scanning the surface of the water. They didn't see any whales, but they both became startlingly aware of their closeness and the lack of any outside influence to interrupt that togetherness. Without any words, they turned away from the bluff and returned to their picnic.

Cassie set out plates and food while Trent opened the bottle of wine and poured each of them a glass. He raised his glass toward her and looked into her green eyes. "To a generous, gracious, and beautiful woman who has been casting a spell over me from the moment we met. To a woman who has forced me to reconsider my life and think about changes."

A flush of embarrassment covered her cheeks at the same time confusion entered her eyes. He should not have said what he did. He had revealed too much. But once the words had escaped into the open, he couldn't take them back.

He had missed seeing her during the day, missed hearing her voice, missed the spirited glint that came into her eyes when annoyed with him. He liked the way she stood up for herself, asserted her authority rather than deferring to the way he kept trying to take charge of things. In spite of that, he was not a control freak. He didn't have that need to be in control of everything and everyone around him.

He held her gaze for a long moment, then softly caressed her cheek. "I know you don't understand what I said. I'm not sure I do, either." He did clearly understand one thing. He would not be leaving the island as casually as he had originally anticipated.

If he left at all.

Then his thoughts jumped to something else that had been on his mind. He wanted to get a look at Cassie's lease to see exactly how things stood, what legal ramifications had been built into the document. He thought fleetingly about checking into taking the Washington bar exam, so he could practice law in the state and take care of his own legal transactions rather than relying on someone else to fill the role he was totally qualified to handle. But that took time, and he had more immediate needs.

As quickly as his wandering thoughts had turned to business matters, he dismissed them. The nearness of Cassie Brockton and his own growing passion for her seemed to consume everything surrounding him. A passion quickly enveloped him, one that he feared might far exceed a merely physical desire. While they ate their food and drank their wine, he attempted some casual conversation.

"Even though this is the first week of May, we're coming up on a holiday weekend for Memorial Day. Is the island considerably more crowded during the summer? More congestion and traffic?"

"Oh, yes. The peaceful atmosphere of the rest of the year is replaced with increased tourist activity, especially on weekends. There are several vacation homes here belonging to people on the mainland. The straight through ferry from Anacortes that doesn't make a stop on any of the other islands is only a little over an hour of transit time. Makes it an easy weekend getaway. And there is the small airport with commuter flights that connects directly with Seattle."

Cassie shot him a questioning look before continuing. "As you know, I'm from Chicago, but I definitely prefer living here rather than dealing with the big city hassle. How about you? Are from a big city or small town?"

"I've lived in both at one time or another. I certainly enjoy all the amenities of the big city but also appreciate the peace and simplicity of the small town."

"Your...uh...your type of work doesn't restrict where you live?"

"Many small towns have a close proximity to large cities. It gives one the best of both worlds—small town living and the big city for earning that living." He laughed, hoping it didn't sound forced or artificial. "This is beginning to sound like my conversation with Jake...lots of questions. But I guess that's normal when two people are getting to know each other."

Her smile totally captivated him. Her laugh sent little ripples of excitement racing down his spine. Everything about her enchanted him while at the same time tugging on the strings that tied his secrets, threatening to expose them.

Cassie sensed Trent's reluctance to talk about himself, to reveal any personal information, so she chose to stay away from specific questions even though she desperately wanted to know everything about him. She wanted to know exactly with whom she just might be falling in love.

As preposterous as that seemed, as improbable as it could be in such a short time, that precisely described what she feared could be happening. She suspected she might have started falling in love with him one minute after she fell off the ladder and into his arms. Their first kiss at his bedroom door had done nothing to dispel that notion despite her words at the time.

She had tried to fight off a specific train of thought but finally allowed one of the thoughts to seep into her consciousness, thoughts about his real feelings for her. Did he consider her just another woman, one in a long line of many he had met during his wanderings? Another woman who had been totally seduced by his charming manner? Did he really care for her? If all he wanted was another sexual conquest, he had passed up a sure bet when he didn't take advantage of her after carrying her upstairs to her bedroom. The fact that he hadn't taken advantage of her spoke to his integrity and trustworthiness.

The words he had uttered when he proposed the toast lingered in her mind, repeating over and over. She wanted so much for them to be true.

Her thoughts quickly vanished in the sensual fire of his lips when he leaned his face into hers. All her doubts, concerns, and apprehensions disappeared as she responded to his kiss. The kiss continued, instilling an even greater desire to know him so much better than mere kisses, a desire that hit her with a jolt of panic. Reluctantly, she broke the tantalizing kiss.

She searched his eyes, seeking answers to her unasked questions, not sure she really wanted to know the truth.

Trent saw the conflict in Cassie's eyes. Had he pushed her too much? Moved too quickly? Nothing in his experience had prepared him for what had been happening since he wandered into her restaurant. Even though he had his luxury yacht docked at the harbor, he rented a room in her house that he didn't need. He had maneuvered his way into her life through deceit with an agenda he could not share with her, one he didn't even have clear in his own mind. But his ultimate goal... He had convinced himself that the end justified the means. How many people had used that excuse to justify bad, unethical, and even illegal actions? He cared about her. He cared very much, perhaps too much. The last thing he wanted was to hurt her.

They sat next to each other on the picnic blanket. It had been a delightful time. Despite his concerns about his deception, Trent felt very comfortable with Cassie, very content. "Tell me...did you acquire your knowledge about Orcas after you moved here, or was it an interest of yours before that?"

"Actually, it's both. When I was a little girl, we would visit Aunt Sofie for one week each year. I always looked forward to that. She was a wonderful person, so full of life. She'd tell me stories about her youth, about her adventures before she finally decided to settle down here on the island." Her face became animated as she talked about Sofie, laughing as she recalled some of her fond memories of the times.

"She led a very full life but never married. We were her only family, at least blood relatives. She was my father's aunt, actually my great aunt." She paused, a tender expression enveloping her features. "She would always say her friends here were family. And now that I live here, I understand what she meant."

He reached over and squeezed her hand. "It sounds like you had a great childhood."

"What about you…your childhood?"

"I'd call it a normal childhood. My father was a financial advisor, and my mother was a nurse. She retired when I came along." A fond memory flashed through his mind. "She would always read me a bedtime story when I was a small child, no matter what. I don't think she missed even one night until I got too old for bedtime stories."

He watched her as she talked, as she laughed. She embodied exactly what he had always wanted—an intelligent, independent woman totally without phony airs and pretenses.

Trent captured her mouth again, then folded her in the warmth of his embrace. He twined his fingers in her hair, caressed her back and shoulders. He did not understand how she had become so important to his life, so important to him, in such a short period of time. It had been a brief few days, yet it felt as if he had known her a lifetime.

Could his emotions be getting away from him? Escalating faster than he could handle? How could he allow it to happen, especially knowing her feelings about attorneys? And what about his deception? Would it only go to reinforce her negative opinion of attorneys and drive her away? And what would happen if she discovered his plans and his intentions before he had all the pieces in place and was ready to divulge them? Too many questions and no answers.

He dismissed his concerns, preferring to dwell on the present rather than speculate about the uncertainties of the future. He darted his tongue into the dark corners of her mouth, reveling in her delicious taste.

He slowly sank to the ground, pulling her with him. The late afternoon sun warmed their skin. A gentle breeze wafted across their bodies, tickling their senses with the clean ocean air. Loose tendrils of her hair fluttered across her face until he smoothed the strands out of the way. It felt as if they existed in a world of their own, apart from any other reality.

Trent wrestled with his uncertainty about how far to take the sensual heat building between them. Even though alone on the bluff, they could be seen by anyone on the road. He didn't want to cause her any concern or embarrassment. But on the other hand, he wanted much more of her than just the kisses they had shared.

Trent broke off the kiss. He cradled her head against his shoulder and held her in his arms. He felt her closeness as she lay stretched out next to him, her arm across his chest. He continued to hold her, gently caressing her cheek and stroking her hair. She felt so right in his arms as if she belonged there.

Cassie snuggled her head into Trent's shoulder.

Even through his shirt, his taut, muscular chest sent tingles rippling from her fingertips through her body. She wanted more of him, but this certainly was not the place to pursue those feelings. She closed her eyes, a smile curling the corners of her lips as she moved her hand across his chest and along the side of his neck before running her fingers through his thick hair.

They stayed together, wrapped in each other's arms, neither feeling any need to speak as late afternoon became evening. The sun dipped toward the horizon. The breeze turned cool.

Trent pulled Cassie closer, sharing his warmth as he spoke. "It's getting cool out here. If you shift your weight a little I can get the edge of the blanket wrapped around your shoulders."

"Actually—" She reluctantly wiggled out of his embrace. "—it's probably time to start back."

Their eyes met, the incendiary look that passed between them unmistakable. She experienced the pull of his magnetism as she melted back into the warmth of his arms. The passion of his kiss again consumed her, inflaming her desires.

Dusk settled around them before they finally gathered their picnic things and started back. Their conversation light and casual, they spoke as old friends would, old friends who were very comfortable with each other.

"There's a movie on television tonight, one of my all-time favorite comedies. If the bar's not too busy, and Mike doesn't need any help, maybe we could watch it together."

"Oh?" His blue eyes sparkled with amusement. "And just what's the name of this all-time favorite comedy? Maybe I've already seen it?"

"You probably have." She shot him a teasing grin. "But you'll want to see it again."

He laughed. "Okay, I'm adequately intrigued."

"*Some Like It Hot* with Tony Curtis, Jack Lemon, and Marilyn Monroe."

"You're right. That is a good one."

She paused as they walked up the path to her house. "I need to check in with Mike to make sure everything is okay."

"Wouldn't he have called you if he had any problems?"

A spontaneous chuckle escaped her throat. "Not necessarily. He likes to think there isn't anything he can't handle."

Trent went to the house while Cassie made an appearance in the bar. The number of customers had Mike dashing around like crazy trying to keep up with it all. She immediately took over waiting tables, but things remained very busy.

Half an hour later, she spotted Trent at the front door. She paused long enough for a few words. "Mike's been swamped, so I stayed to help."

"So I see. I wondered what happened—"

She rushed off to deliver some drinks before he could finish his sentence. Warmth filled her when he stepped behind the bar to help Mike. Even though she had been angry with him on more than one occasion for butting into her business, this time she truly appreciated the fact that he had chosen to ignore her admonishments.

He started by washing the backlog of dirty glasses, then refilling the ice bins and icing down bottles of the most popular brands of beer. Mike didn't say anything, but his expression showed his gratitude for the volunteered help, even though it came from an unwelcome source. Business stayed brisk until closing.

Cassie locked the door and put out the *Closed* sign after the last customer departed. "Whew! That was quite a rush." She plopped down on a bar stool. "There should be some good totals on the register."

"Here." Trent handed her a glass of wine. "Sit down and relax for a minute." He grabbed a bottle of beer from the ice and held it up toward Mike with a questioning look. "How about you?"

Trent opened it as Mike nodded his head in agreement while ringing out the totals on the register. Trent started to pour himself a glass of wine, then changed his mind. Instead, he poured himself a draft beer.

"Thanks." Mike picked up the cold beer and took a long swig directly from the bottle. "That hits the spot." He handed the cash register tape to Cassie. "Definitely a good night's business."

She suppressed the smile that tried to curl the corners of her mouth. Jake had obviously had that talk with Mike, just as he promised. Mike was making a genuine effort to be friendly with Trent, or at least Mike's version of friendly. Trent's gesture of joining Mike with a beer rather than a glass of wine did not escape her notice, either. Everything seemed so perfect.

She listened as the two men made an earnest attempt at friendly conversation.

"What type of activities are there here? Do you play golf?

"Naw, golfin' ain't my game." Mike gestured

toward the dart board in a side alcove. "Do you play darts?"

"I tried it once in a pub in England." He furrowed his brow in a moment's concentration. "How about bicycling?"

The topic they finally settled on was fishing.

Mike's face became animated as he told Trent about his best catch. "Yeah, I once landed a twenty pound Coho, three feet long."

"Really? That's quite a prize. I thought Coho salmon were in the eight to twelve pound range, twenty-four to thirty inches long.

"Yeah, that's about what they usually run. But Jake and me was havin' a really lucky day."

As they warmed to their discussion, Cassie went around the bar to the register to count out the cash drawer. Normally, she would remove the cash drawer from the register and count it out in her office, but she didn't want to bring a halt to Mike's attempt to make friends with Trent.

Trent saw the perplexed look on her face as she stared at the money piled on the bar, the bills neatly stacked next to the coins. She went through them again, counting every last penny. The furrow in her brow deepened as she stared at the money.

"What's the matter?" Trent circled around behind the bar and stood next to her. "Is something wrong?"

"The cash drawer is short." She lifted the front of the cash drawer from where it fit into the register and looked under it but didn't see anything. "It's short by exactly fifty dollars. That's quite a bit and odd that it would be an exact amount like that rather than an odd amount of dollars and cents."

Mike was there immediately. "There's nothing under the cash drawer? I took in a fifty-dollar bill from Jim Spencer. He wanted change. I shoved it under the drawer just like I do with anything over a twenty, along with any checks and credit card receipts." He shot a hard look at Trent, then returned his attention to Cassie. "Do you have any fifties there in the stacks?" He indicated the wrapped bills stacked on the bar.

"No, no fifties at all." She picked up the wrapped stacks of bills and carefully sifted through them, looking at the denomination of each bill in hopes that she had stuck the fifty in with the twenties. "Nope, no fifty."

"What happened to it?" Mike glared at Trent, his accusation unmistakable.

"I wouldn't know since I never saw it." Trent glared back, not quite sure what to do. He understood Mike's suspicion falling on him. He also believed there wasn't any reason to suspect Mike of having taken it, unless Mike had purposely attempted to discredit him.

Trent dismissed that notion as being too ridiculous to pursue. Maybe back home that would have been a viable thought, but not here on the island. Besides, Mike didn't seem to be a devious or underhanded person. He came right out with his thoughts and was up front with his feelings.

"It has to be here somewhere." Trent squatted down, looked under the bar and searched the surrounding floor area. "Maybe down here." He moved things around, looking behind bottles. But after a thorough search he came up empty-handed.

Again, Mike glared at Trent, then turned toward Cassie. "I know I shoved a fifty dollar bill under the cash drawer. Things were hectic, and I was rushed, but I'm sure of the denomination of the bill—definitely a fifty and not a twenty. Even if I made a mistake and gave him change for a fifty when he gave me a twenty, the drawer would be off by thirty dollars, not fifty. And Jim Spencer would have been honest about it and returned the overage."

Trent turned to Cassie, his voice and manner calm. "I can't explain what happened"—he shot a pointed look at Mike—"but I can understand that you would automatically suspect me. After all, I am a stranger who has only been here for a few days. If it will settle this matter, even though I did not touch the cash register at any time this evening, I'll replace the money if that will put an end to it." He held her gaze, his face reflecting open honesty.

She quickly stepped between the two men. "Cut it out, both of you. I'm not accusing anyone of stealing. There has to be another explanation, some logical reason for the drawer being fifty dollars short. Now, I don't want to hear any more about it tonight." Her attitude didn't show any anger, just very authoritative and businesslike. She made no accusations or excuses. "Mike, put the money back into the cash drawer, then take the drawer out of the register. Trent, make sure the front door is locked and turn out the lights. This bar is now officially closed for today."

Trent did as instructed. His analytical mind tried to sort out what had happened and what to do about it. The amount of money, fifty dollars, had no particular meaning to him—small change by his standards. A mere pittance. More troublesome than the missing money? The exchange of words that had just taken place and the tension filling the air. The last thing he wanted was for Cassie to have doubts and concerns about his continued presence.

Mike lifted the front of the cash drawer and pressed the release that allowed it to be removed from the register drawer. He scowled as he tried it again. The mechanism seemed to be jammed. He closed the register drawer and opened it again, then made another try at removing the inner cash drawer.

Cassie and Trent both became aware of Mike's struggle. "What's the matter?" Cassie quickly moved toward the register while Trent chose to keep his distance.

"I don't know. The release is caught on something. The drawer won't lift out." Mike removed the money and stacked it on the bar again. Then, for five minutes, he shoved, wiggled, and tugged at the release on the cash drawer. After uttering a string of obscenities, Mike finally worked the release free and the cash drawer slid out of the register. He stood with the cash drawer in his hands, staring at the release mechanism at the back of the register drawer.

Mike set the cash drawer on the bar, reached into the back of the register and withdrew a mangled piece of paper. He smoothed it out on the bar—a torn and crumpled fifty dollar bill.

Embarrassment flashed across Mike's face as his sheepish gaze darted from Cassie to Trent, then back to Cassie.

Trent quickly spoke up before Mike could say anything. "There…I knew the problem had a logical explanation. Now, we can all call it a night and get some sleep."

Mike shifted his weight uncomfortably. "Look, uh, I guess I was a little quick—"

"Good night, Mike." Trent cut off his words with an upbeat tone and a friendly smile as he walked toward the back door.

Both Cassie and Mike watched Trent leave, then she picked up the cash drawer as she eyed Mike. "Well?"

"Come on, Cassie." His expression took on that of a child who had been caught in some mischief and tried to make it seem not really that bad. "What was I supposed to think?"

"You were supposed to think that there must be some logical explanation. Trent has handled the money both here and in the restaurant since he arrived. It would have been so easy for him to steal it before he rang it on the register tape, especially when he worked your bar shift and was here alone when you were sick. If he doesn't register the sale, he can pocket the customer's money. He's not so stupid that he would steal from your register after the amount had been rung up." She stood patiently, waiting to see what Mike had to say.

"Yeah, I guess you're right. Now I suppose you're gonna want me to apologize to him or somethin'?"

"You do whatever you think is right, but in case you didn't notice, Trent just graciously let you off the hook."

Mike allowed a sheepish grin. "Yeah, I noticed."

Cassie gave him an affectionate hug before turning to leave, indicating that all was forgiven. "Good night, Mike. See you tomorrow."

She took the cash drawer and went through the

back door, leaving him to finish locking up. After she entered her house, she paused at the foot of the staircase. The light coming from beneath Trent's door indicated he was still up. She rapped lightly on the door. After a moment, it opened, the light flooding into the darkened hallway.

She started to speak. Before she could say anything Trent reached out and ran his fingertips seductively across her cheek. He twined his fingers in her hair, then drew her to him. With his other hand, he took the cash drawer from her and set it on the nightstand by his bed. He enfolded her in his embrace, holding her against his body. He did not try to kiss her, just held her close.

The warmth and strength of his embrace titillated her senses. She hadn't intended this when she knocked on his door. Her purpose had been to apologize for the incident over the fifty dollars. She had intended only to say a few words, then go up to her room.

Those intentions disappeared in a heartbeat, a very excited heartbeat.

She tried once again to speak, mustering all her self-control. "I only wanted to apologize." Her words, muffled in his chest, seemed to be drowned out by the sound of his strong heartbeat.

"There's nothing to apologize for." His soft voice emulated a tender caress. "An honest mistake. I've already forgotten it."

Reluctantly, she pulled away from his warm embrace. "Thank you. That's very gracious of you...considering the circumstances. Now, I'd better get to sleep."

She picked up the cash drawer, left his room, and shut the door behind her.

****

At ten-thirty the next morning, Trent finally made an appearance at the restaurant to have breakfast. No sooner had Cassie served his food than Mike entered. Rather than going directly to the bar, he slowly made his way to Trent's booth.

He awkwardly shifted his weight from one foot to the other as he stood there.

"Listen, uh, about yesterday—"

"Hey, don't worry about it, Mike. An honest mistake. No harm done. It's forgotten." Trent flashed a sincere smile and returned his attention to his breakfast. Mike continued to watch him for a minute longer before going to the bar to start his shift.

Trent had not fallen asleep easily last night. His mind had been clouded with confusion. He wanted Cassie. He wanted her very much. He also wanted to be honest with her. If only he knew what the outcome of that honesty would be. If only he had some type of guarantee that the truth would not alienate her.

He woke early that morning and had put in a busy day even before going to breakfast. His thoughts had been dominated by his plans for the future. As soon as he had showered and dressed, he went directly to Cassie's office while she was at work, his intention being to find a copy of her lease agreement with Bob Hampton. He had searched through all her files and finally found it. Giving the legal document a quick read, one particular section caught his attention. He had carefully gone back over it a second time.

He couldn't stop the smile of satisfaction that turned the corners of his mouth. He used Cassie's printer-copier to make a copy of the entire document, then returned the lease to where he found it. He had no doubts about Cassie being unaware of the specific provisions of the lease. And if Bob Hampton knew the specifics of what the lease contained, his correspondence with Randall Davies would have been of a much different nature.

Next, he had called Randall Davies. "That's what's in the lease. I'll send you a copy. It's a sure bet that neither Cassie Brockton nor Bob Hampton know the specific parameters of the agreement. Now that we have the missing pieces, I need you to get started on what we discussed…get it set up as quickly as you can."

Trent lingered over breakfast, sharing quick bits of conversation with Cassie as she took care of other customers. She introduced him to Charlene, a pleasant woman in her forties. Following breakfast, he settled himself into the porch swing, leaned back, and let out a sigh of contentment. He felt very good about the business arrangements he and Randall had discussed. Very good, indeed, with everything falling into place nicely.

His gaze wandered across the horizon. He took in the breathtaking view, the open water dotted with a myriad of forested islands—some inhabited, some privately owned, some devoid of human population, and some no larger than a dot on the horizon. He felt so relaxed and comfortable knowing he had made the right decision in wanting to stay. He spotted Cassie on the path and put his thoughts on hold as he watched her walk toward the house.

He motioned for her to join him on the swing. "Busy day?"

As he moved over to make room for her to sit

down, he took the cash drawer and the ledgers from her and set them on the porch.

"Busy enough, but not too bad. With Mike and Charlene both back, things have returned to a normal routine. What have you been up to?"

"I spent some time reading this morning, and since breakfast, I've just been sitting here enjoying the clean air and the beautiful view." His voice grew very soft, very sensual. "What do you plan to do with the rest of today?"

"This is my busiest office day. I need to place my supply orders for both the restaurant and the bar, and it's the day I do payroll."

"I see." He slipped his hand along the side of her face, then twined his fingers in her hair. "Could I entice you to join me right here this evening for a glass of wine?"

"Mmm, I wouldn't be surprised to find that you could entice me to do just about anything you wanted."

Chapter Six

Thoughts of Cassie filled Trent's mind. Her words about readily agreeing to anything he wanted played over and over through his consciousness. He left the porch and wandered back to the bar where a dozen or so patrons watched a baseball game on television. He took a seat at the bar, ordered a beer, and half-heartedly watched the game while making occasional small talk with Mike who seemed to still be trying to apologize.

Trent quickly lost interest in the baseball game. He picked up a copy of the local newspaper, scanned the real estate ads, and marked several properties for sale—both business and residential.

Jake's good-natured laugh and friendly greeting filled the room as he came through the door. He immediately spotted Trent and took a seat next to him. He indicated the television. "What's the score, and what inning are they in?"

Trent's embarrassed smile said it all. "I haven't the slightest idea." He placed the newspaper on the bar. "I'm not really paying any attention to the game."

With Jake around, things seldom stayed quiet for long. In a matter of minutes, he had the entire bar involved in a discussion about football. As Jake explained to Trent, "Baseball's boring, football's exciting."

The conversation quickly segued from sports to

fishing, a topic the locals seemed to prefer.

"If you don't have any plans for tomorrow, would you like to go out with me in the morning?" Jake tilted his head and extended a friendly smile. "Fishing's a great way to get to know someone. We'll do a little fishing and exchange opinions on how to run the world in a more efficient manner."

Trent considered Jake's offer for a moment. "I'd like that. Let's do it."

"Good. We'll meet for breakfast at five o'clock, then go from there." After finalizing arrangements for the next morning, Jake excused himself and left to do errands. Trent left the bar shortly after Jake.

Trent wandered into town and walked the streets, finally arriving at a real estate office. He looked at the photographs and read the descriptions of properties for sale. He continued to explore the town, making note of the various types of business including which ones seemed seasonal and which ones year-round.

He went into the bookstore and browsed for a while, then wandered into a combination art gallery and gift shop. This particular business caught his eye because the merchandise appeared to be of superior quality rather than typical tourist trinkets and T-shirts. One painting, in particular, immediately grabbed his full attention.

He thought back to the night he had carried Cassie up to her bedroom. He visualized the interior of the room. Unlike the rest of the house, it did not feel like someone's maiden aunt. It also had a sensuality to it, reflecting the woman who slept there. The colors were soft, muted shades with an occasional splash of a particularly vivid hue to bring everything alive.

The color and feel of the painting exactly matched her bedroom. He wanted to buy the painting as a present for her, so he paid for it and had the gallery hold it for him. Pleased with his find, he returned to Cassie's house.

****

Cassie entered the bar and selected a good bottle of red wine. Before she could leave, Mike pulled a newspaper from beneath the counter and handed it to her.

She looked at him questioningly. "What's the significance of this?"

"Trent marked up this newspaper. Don't you think this is strange?"

She again furrowed her brow in concentration. Why would Trent be marking local properties and businesses for sale? She slowly shook her head as she continued to stare at the newspaper. *Very perplexing.* It raised one more question about Trent Nichols and the reason for his presence on her island.

"I still don't trust him, Cassie. Okay, I was wrong about the fifty-dollar bill, but I still think there's something wrong about him. Have you thought about this? He could be a con man after your money."

Cassie couldn't stop the laugh. "Really, Mike? A con man?"

"I *know* he's hidin' somethin'. You need to be more cautious around him, make sure he doesn't have access to your business records."

"I appreciate your concern, but I think you're way off base. The idea of him being after my money…well, it doesn't make any sense. I make enough to pay all my bills with a little left over for savings, but that's a long way from having enough to be the target of a con man."

She took the bottle of wine and returned to her house. After opening the bottle, she placed it on the table next to the porch swing along with two glasses.

She watched as Trent walked up the path from the street, and just the sight of him caused her growing emotional attachment to well up, shoving aside all doubts and concerns. As soon as he spotted her, he smiled and waved. She returned his wave and held up an empty wine glass. He hurried the few remaining steps to the porch swing.

"Is this ready to pour?" He picked up the bottle and one of the glasses.

"Yes, you're just in time."

He poured a glass for each of them, then held his glass toward her. "To you, Cassie. A lovely lady who fills my every thought."

She sipped her wine, their gazes locked in a highly sensual moment, then turned her gaze to the ocean view.

"How did you spend your day while I was working?"

"I went to the bar. Everybody was watching a baseball game. Since I'm not really much of a baseball fan, I read the newspaper. Then Jake came in." He chuckled softly. "He certainly gets things going, a very addictive personality. Within minutes, he had everyone engaged in a conversation about football."

Cassie joined his laughter. "Yes, indeed. That's Jake. He gets everyone involved in something. And he is much more of a football fan than baseball. However, his favorite group topic is usually fishing."

"Not surprising. We're going fishing in the

morning. I'm meeting him at the restaurant for breakfast at five o'clock."

"She chuckled. "Well, when Jake says five o'clock, he doesn't mean five minutes after five."

"Yes, he strikes me as that type of person."

They sipped their wine, the porch swing gently swaying back and forth. He put his arm around her shoulders. "It looks like we're going to have another beautiful sunset tonight. It must be really nice to enjoy this beautiful view all year."

"This is May. This time of year through summer, the sunset happens later at night. In winter, sunset occurs in late afternoon. Even when we visited Aunt Sofie and I was only a child, this porch swing was always my favorite place at her house."

"I can see why. It's very relaxing and peaceful here."

"What else did you do this afternoon? What did you discover in our little town?"

"It's a nice *little town*. I found a couple of interesting art galleries."

"I love art galleries and museums. Monet is my favorite artist. In fact, I love all kinds of museums. That was one thing I liked about living in Chicago—lots of great museums."

He had never mentioned any type of a job and had side-stepped the moment during their picnic when she had broached the subject of his employment. She had no idea of how he could afford to spend an indefinite period of time on the island without concern for returning to his home and his work. And he had paid her for the room for a month in advance…in cash.

Her mind kept going back to the newspaper Mike

had shown her, back to the question of why he would be checking on real estate and businesses for sale. A thought tried to brighten the uncertainty that had settled over her. Could he be looking for a means of supporting himself so he would be able to stay for good? Dare she hope, to stay with her?

Cassie screwed up her courage and hesitantly voiced her concerns. "Trent?"

He kissed her on the forehead. "Yes?"

"This afternoon…in the bar…"

"What's wrong?"

She sat upright. "What do you do…for a living, I mean? Are you in real estate?"

His expression changed to one of surprise. "Real estate? What makes you ask that?"

"Well…" She swallowed, trying to chase away the tightness in her throat. "This afternoon in the bar, you marked several local businesses along with some other properties listed for sale in the newspaper. Is that why you're here? To…" Almost afraid to say the words out loud, she finally forced them into the open. "Uh, to buy some local business?"

She had not actually formulated her exact fears until that moment. What if he was on the island for the purpose of buying out Bob Hampton? Jake had said the two men obviously didn't know each other, but that didn't mean Trent had no interest in buying the property from him. Her voice quavered, and her body began to tremble. "Are you here to help Bob Hampton take my business away from me?"

Trent heard her words along with the fear and anxiety in her voice. How could he answer her question? He took a calming breath and closed his eyes for a moment, trying to compose his thoughts. "A friend of mine in Seattle was contacted by Bob Hampton. My friend, who had never heard of Bob Hampton before receiving his letter, thought the letter sounded vague and suspicious in addition to very confusing. He asked me if I would mind stopping here and checking into the situation for him. As a result of my report, my friend decided that he did not want to involve himself in whatever Bob Hampton had in mind."

"Oh…" Her expression brightened, as if a huge weight had just been lifted from her shoulders. "So that's the only reason you're here?"

"No. That's the reason I came here, not the reason I stayed. I called my friend with the information he wanted the first day I was here, before I had my brief and unpleasant encounter with Bob Hampton at the restaurant, which confirmed the thoughts and feelings I conveyed to my friend." He cupped her face in his hands and searched the depths of her eyes. "I stayed because I found a delightful woman that I wanted to get to know much better."

He knew he had not told her everything, that he had purposely bent the truth and twisted the reality of the situation. However, until Randall Davies had finalized Trent's instructions, there wasn't anything else he could say, except one thing. "Cassie, I would never purposely do anything to hurt you. You're very important to me."

She rose from the swing, her voice thick with desire despite her words to the contrary. "It's getting late, and we both have to be up early. I have a restaurant to open, and you have a fishing trip with

Jake."

"I know." He walked with her to the front door and opened it so she could enter. "Good night, Cassie."

He softly brushed his lips against hers with tender, loving concern rather than passion, then turned and entered the house through the door into his bedroom. He wanted to make sure that appearances did not compromise Cassie's reputation.

Trent quickly undressed and climbed into bed. His body ached with his desire for her. His need to answer her fears with only half truths bothered him. What a tricky double-edged sword. He wanted to make love to her, openly and passionately. On the other side, he was not able to be honest with her about who he was or his undeclared intentions.

He had given it a lot of thought, a whole new direction for his talents and energies. Too many things circulated through his head—problems, hopes, desires, new plans, possibilities for the future. As soon as he closed his eyes, a vision of Cassie played across his consciousness. He shoved all thoughts aside...all but one.

****

Upstairs, Cassie sat on the edge of her bed, her thoughts a tangled mass of confusion. Tremors began in the pit of her stomach and radiated outward. She had made her decision. She only hoped she wasn't making a fool of herself. Trent said he would never hurt her, and she believed him. She undressed, showered, then prepared to go to his room. She slipped into her robe and ran a brush through her hair. Butterflies flitted inside her stomach. Her pulse raced as she paused to check her appearance in the mirror. Was she about to make a colossal mistake?

The soft knock at her bedroom door startled her. When she opened the door, dim light from her bedroom spilled out into the dark hallway, highlighting Trent's taut nearly nude body and handsome face. Her gaze met his in a long, heated moment as she stared into the smoldering blue intensity of his eyes, then she stepped aside. Her voice contained neither hesitation nor uncertainty. "Come in."

He grasped her hand as he entered her bedroom, then pulled her into his embrace. He caressed her back and shoulders as he buried his face in her hair. Pulling back slightly, he looked deeply into her eyes while gently cupping her face in his hands. "I want to make love to you. I want this very much. I hope you do, too."

With all the passion stored inside her, she uttered one breathless word. "Yes."

No other words needed to be spoken. She loved him. The crystal clear reality jumped into her consciousness. No more uncertainty. No more questioning. She could not explain it, did not understand how it could have happened so quickly, but she knew it to be true.

His arms tightened around her, the heat of his intensity flooding inside her. Her fingers caressed the taut muscles of his back and shoulders. Her lips lightly brushed across his bare shoulder, then traced against his chest.

Trent dropped the condom packets he brought with him on top of the nightstand next to her bed, then his nimble fingers moved quickly to untie the sash at her waist. He dropped it to the floor, then slowly ran his hands inside her robe as he bent his head to capture her mouth. After wrapping his arms around her, his fingers tickled across her back.

Cassie trembled with excitement as he slipped the robe off her shoulders and let it drop to the floor on top of the sash. His mouth captured hers, his tongue darting and twining seductively. The force of his masculinity nearly overwhelmed her as she melted into him, giving in to all the passion he stirred in her. She pressed the fullness of her breasts against his body as he cupped the perfect roundness of her bare bottom.

She slid her hands down his back, tucked them inside the elastic band of his briefs, then tugged. She slowly lowered them below his hips until his hardened arousal sprang free of the confining fabric. She had never before been so bold, so aggressive. But then, no one had ever excited her the way Trent did, certainly not her ex-husband.

He released her just long enough to discard his briefs. With one smooth maneuver, he laid her back on the softness of the bed and stretched his body out next to hers.

Her breathing became erratic, matching his ragged gasps. He smoothed her hair back from her face as he again captured her mouth in a frenzy of heated passion that curled her toes. His fingers stroked the length of her body, traced the outline of her hip, then came to rest on the fullness of her breast. He tempted and teased the tautly pebbled nipple with his fingers, then with his tongue, before taking it into his mouth. She emitted little moans of pleasure as he gently sucked.

She ran her fingers through his thick, dark blond hair as she rubbed her foot along the edge of his bare calf. She had known making love with Trent would be every bit this wonderful, every bit this thrilling. She caressed his shoulders and back, lowering her fingers occasionally to tickle across his bottom cheek.

He quickly moved to suck her other breast as his hands stroked the smooth skin of her inner thighs. A delicious shudder shot through her body and settled low in the heated center of her core. His fingers twirled through the downy softness between her thighs and slowly slipped through the moist folds into her body.

Her whimper of delight died in her throat when his mouth came down hard on hers, his labored breathing matching her own. She had never before felt the level of excitement he created in her, experienced the intensity of the all-consuming passion that coursed through her veins at that moment.

He continued to titillate her body with his sensual mouth, tasting the valley nestled between her breasts, kissing her stomach, running his tongue around her navel, and moving to her abdomen. His hot breath came in short, ragged gasps as his lips teased the sensitive skin of her inner thighs. She instantly responded with a sharp intake of air followed by a soft, sensual moan.

He found her hot moist core, eliciting shudders and throaty gasps of unbridled passion as he tasted her delicate femininity. She arched toward him, demanding and receiving more of his sensual ministrations. Then, from deep inside, wave after wave of explosive ecstasy welled up and swept through her body, the surging tide taking her by surprise with its suddenness. It continued beyond her wildest expectations. Finally, the waves subsided.

It had never happened like that before. Never had she arrived at the pinnacle of ecstasy so quickly and effortlessly. Granted, it had been a long time since she had enjoyed the attentions of a desirable man. In fact, not since she had moved to the island. But never had lovemaking started out on such a high level. It was the type of thing she scoffed at in romance novels, a sensual touch to just the right spot producing instant orgasmic bliss between two people who barely knew each other, who had only a physical attraction. It just didn't happen that way in real life.

But despite the improbability, it had just happened. It happened to her. And she reveled in the splendor. Another truth she had to face. It was not just sex. It had also been a long time since she had been involved in an emotional relationship.

Then a cloud obscured her thought. The concept of a relationship, did it exist only in her mind? A wish not shared by Trent?

He gently cupped and caressed the fullness of her breasts, instantly pulling her out of her thoughts and back into the sensuality of Trent Nichols. She basked in the moment as he provocatively ran his fingers through the downy softness of her triangle while whispering in her ear. "I want to give you more pleasure again and again."

No one had ever said that to her before, verbally expressed a concern for her pleasure and needs rather than only his desires. She ran her hands over his hard-muscled chest, tickling her fingers through the wisps of sandy-colored hair. Her hands lingered here and there as she bestowed little kisses and nibbles on his shoulders and across his chest. Her fingers reached down for his erection, softly caressing and stroking his hardened arousal. She again lost herself in his delicious lovemaking, his bare skin against hers, the sensations created by his electrifying touch.

Trent quickly grabbed one of the condom packets and sheathed his erection. He inserted his knee between her thighs as she opened herself to receive him. He poised his body above hers, then slowly penetrated her as a low, throaty growl escaped his lips. He consumed the sweetness of her mouth while setting a slow, smooth rhythm. Their hips moved in perfect unison. They were so in sync, each attuned to the wants and needs of the other. The intensity of his strokes increased, their thrusting accelerated. The shared sensations built to a fever pitch, then their incendiary passions exploded.

They abandoned themselves to wanton desires. His muscles tensed as she dug her fingers into the firm flesh of his rear end. A shudder moved through his body as he gave a final deep plunge inside her.

Time teetered on the brink of infinity. She gasped, her inner muscles rhythmically grabbing and tugging his rigid shaft, a sensation that generated his hard spasms of release. They were completely spent, skin glistening with beads of perspiration, arms and legs tangled together, bodies exhausted. He brushed a loose tendril of hair from her damp cheek, then placed a soft kiss there as he tenderly enfolded her in his warm embrace.

They lay quietly, enveloped in the cocoon that surrounded the afterglow of their lovemaking. He didn't speak. He didn't want to break the magical spell engulfing them. Slowly, their breathing returned to normal.

The impact of their lovemaking, the emotional

reality of what he felt, hit him hard. He cared about her very much. Perhaps too much? He had a firm business plan in mind, a plan that had already been set in motion. But had he, as she had accused him on more than one occasion, jumped into something he wanted without taking into consideration that he could be messing with her business and her livelihood? Stepping on her toes by not consulting her? Would she end up being so angry with him this time that he wouldn't be able to smooth over the situation? He had figured all the angles and ramifications and knew it would be to her advantage as well as his, but would she be able to see that through an emotional reaction?

She rested her head against his chest, drawing his attention away from his disturbing thoughts and concerns. He twined his fingers in her hair with one hand while gently stroking down her back and across her bottom with the other. She closed her eyes as she snuggled her body next to his. In a matter of only moments her slow, even breathing told him she had fallen asleep.

He didn't have quite as easy a time of it. There were so many things he wanted to say to her, so many feelings and emotions he wanted to share. Most of all, he wanted to be honest with her. He didn't want any deceptions to stand in the way of what he knew was his growing emotional involvement with her.

He looked at her as she lay sleeping in his arms. Each passing hour dug him deeper and deeper into the hole he had created with his deception. He had to figure some way of getting out of it without losing her. He placed a tender kiss on her forehead, gently pulled her closer to him, and closed his eyes.

****

Trent woke with a start the next morning as the cold air hit his skin. Just moments before, Cassie had nestled next to him. He reached out and grabbed her wrist, pulling her back as she tried to quietly slip out of bed. In a voice thick with sleep, he managed a few words. "What time is it?"

"It's four in the morning and I have to be at work in forty-five minutes." The warmth of her body as he grasped her wrist tingled through him.

He focused on her as the fuzziness of sleep cleared from his head. "You can spare five minutes." He enfolded her in his embrace. All the tender feelings and heated passions of the night before surged through his body.

Everything about her excited him. So exquisite, so delightful, so open and honest in her response. He liked touching her, feeling the silkiness of her skin, kissing her. And now he could add making love with her to that list. He also liked simply talking to her, sitting on the porch swing sharing a glass of wine. Just being with her.

All Cassie's desires instantly jumped to life the moment Trent's fingers had wrapped around her wrist and she heard his thick, sleepy words. A shiver darted up her spine when his tongue teased her nipple to a taut peak. "I don't have five…" A soft moan escaped her throat. "Well, no more than five minutes."

Her breathing quickened. Her eyes closed, and a smile curled the corners of her mouth. She wrapped her arms around his neck and ran her fingers through his tousled hair as she rubbed her foot against his leg.

She needed to put a stop to this all-too-tempting

seduction he had initiated. She needed to get ready for work. She needed to... She did not know what she needed to do. She only knew he totally clouded her better judgment to the point where she could not think straight.

He nuzzled her neck as he rolled her over on top of him and held her tightly. They both lay quietly for a moment longer, his arms wrapped around her and her head resting against his chest.

Finally, Cassie reluctantly broke their moment of reverie. "As delightful as this is, if I don't get out of this bed right now, I'll be late for work."

With an audible sigh of resignation, he released her from his embrace. He kissed her on the cheek, then she quickly slipped out of bed before she again succumbed to his way too tempting touch. She picked up her robe from where it had fallen on the floor the night before, then turned toward the bathroom.

He climbed out after her. "We both have to get moving. I'm meeting Jake at five o'clock."

Trent touched her arm, bringing her to a halt. She turned and caught a moment of eye contact with him, a fleeting glimpse of sadness...or was it regret?

"Trent? What's wrong?"

"Cassie..." He gently caressed her cheek with his fingertips as he continued to gaze into the depths of her green eyes. "There're so many things I need to..."

Trent quickly wrapped his arms around her and drew her to him, burying his face in her hair in order to stop his own words. Not the right time. He couldn't just blurt it out right before they had to part company for several hours. The situation required carefully chosen words so she would understand, so she wouldn't be hurt or angry over his deception, over what he planned to do, over the direction he planned to move in the very near future. He needed to be there to answer her questions and reassure her about that future.

He pulled back from her. "It's getting late. We both need to get going."

****

"Good morning, Jake." Cassie filled his cup with freshly brewed coffee.

"Hi, Cassie." Jake looked around the deserted restaurant. As usual, he had been waiting when she unlocked the door to open for business. "Where's Trent? We're going fishing today. He's supposed to meet me here."

"I'm sure he'll be along any minute. I heard his shower running when I left this morning."

"Good morning, everyone." Trent's voice came from the kitchen as he made his way to the front of the restaurant.

After a quick breakfast, the two men rose to leave. Cassie pulled an envelope out of the cash register and handed it to Trent. "Here, this is for you."

He took the envelope from her, confusion covering his face. He opened it, stared at the check, then looked back at her. "What's this?"

"It's a paycheck for the day you worked in the bar when Mike was sick."

To her surprise, he quickly grabbed her arm and pulled her aside, out of earshot from anyone who might be listening. "You didn't tell me to work or even ask me to work. I volunteered my help. You're not obligated to pay me for those hours. You can't afford to be doing that."

She reached her fingers to the corners of his mouth and turned them up into a smile, then smoothed out the furrow on his brow. "Watch your posterior. You're about to get that swift kick in the seat of the pants. Once again you seem to have forgotten that I'm the owner of this business. You worked the hours, and you should be paid for them." She flashed him a sly grin as she abruptly changed the subject. "Jake's waiting. You'd better get going. He firmly believes that if the boat isn't where he wants to go before seven in the morning the fish will refuse to bite."

He had obviously tried to force a stern look while, at the same time, lovingly caressing her cheek with his fingertips. "We'll discuss this tonight."

Trent joined Jake, and they headed toward the docks. He had a much better day than he had anticipated. Fishing wasn't really one of his favorite things. To his surprise, he found his day with Jake consisted of very little fishing and a great deal of interesting conversation combined with a sightseeing tour around the islands.

When Trent first approached Jake's boat, from a distance it had appeared to be battered and dirty. But once aboard, he found it neat and remarkably clean for a commercial fishing boat. Everything appeared orderly. The installed equipment included the latest in sonar, radar, and radio gear.

Trent felt very comfortable with Jake and surprised at the wide variety of knowledge he possessed. They discussed many topics, exchanging information and differing opinions as part of an intelligent conversation rather than an adversarial confrontation. Jake took him on a seagoing tour around the islands.

"Right here on San Juan Island, at what is now San Juan Island National Historic Park, an incident occurred in 1859 that almost ignited a full blown war between the U.S. and Britain, and it all started with a pig. America and Britain both claimed possession of San Juan Island and each country maintained a presence on the island. An uneasy truce existed until an American farmer shot a British pig he discovered tearing up his potato patch. Because of this, the British tried to arrest the farmer. The farmer called in the local American troops in his support. The British Navy sent three warships and over two thousand men. The American government sent troops. No shots were fired beyond the original shot that killed the pig. San Juan Island eventually became part of the San Juan Islands group that belongs to the United States."

"Is that right?" Trent nodded his head in appreciation of Jake's knowledge.

"Yep."

It was close to noon when Jake swung the boat around and headed back toward home. He navigated into the main channel, the water immediately becoming very choppy due to the large ocean-going vessels using the passageway to travel from the Pacific Ocean to Seattle located on Puget Sound. "Whoa! We must be at the middle of rush hour traffic. This is the choppiest I've ever seen these waters without the help of bad weather."

The rough water buffeted the thirty-five foot boat with increasing regularity as they moved farther out into the main channel. A sudden thud jolted the fishing boat, sending Trent sprawling to the deck as he tried to grab hold of anything to maintain his balance. Jake didn't fare as well. The hard jolt threw him against an open hatch.

Trent quickly scrambled to his feet. Jake, however, couldn't regain his footing. He grabbed his left leg and grimaced in pain. "I think I've broken it."

Without a wasted minute, Trent immediately took control of the situation. "Don't move. Keep your leg immobile. Do you think you can hang on until I get us out of the middle of this channel?"

Jake shot him a dubious look. "Do you think you can handle her okay?"

Trent answered his question with a confident smile. "No problem. You just try to relax and hang on to something so you don't slide around on the deck."

Trent took the controls of the fishing boat and handled it with expert efficiency while flawlessly navigating toward their destination without the help of a chart. And while doing that, he also placed a radio call to have medical help waiting at the harbor when they arrived. As he pulled around the bend and approached the dock, he radioed the harbor master a second time to announce his arrival and confirm the presence of the emergency medical van.

He easily maneuvered the fishing boat into a temporary tie-up position at the pier, then tossed a bow line and stern line to the dockhand, who quickly secured them. He stood aside as the medical technicians came aboard and took Jake off the boat.

As they carried Jake from the boat, the harbor master came up to Trent and spoke in hushed tones. "Uh, Mr. Nichols, this isn't Jake's docking space. This is only for temporary docking. If the boat stays here more than two hours, I'll have to charge him—"

"If there's a problem," he cut in sharply, "put it on my bill." He looked back toward Jake just in time to see Jake's head snap to attention at Trent's words, no mistaking the surprised and curious look on the man's face or the silent question in his eyes.

Trent accompanied them to the emergency medical clinic. He made no mention of the incident, and to his relief, Jake didn't ask any questions. Almost three hours passed before he could take Jake home, the bone only cracked rather than broken. He saw to Jake's comfort, made a quick trip to the pharmacy to fill the prescription the clinic had given him, then moved Jake's boat to its proper docking space.

He glanced at his watch. He had just enough time to get to the gallery and pick up the painting he had purchased yesterday.

Chapter Seven

Trent sat on the edge of Cassie's bed absorbing the overall effect the painting had on the bedroom. He liked it. He liked it very much. He hoped she would, too. He placed a card on her dresser, then left the bedroom.

He returned to his room, removed an empty envelope from the desk drawer, and placed the check she had given him inside it along with all the tip money he had accumulated that same day. He planned to give the tip money to Mike and return the paycheck to Cassie.

He heard Cassie enter the house and go upstairs. The loud shriek reached his ears, followed a minute later by the sound of someone charging down the stairs, then banging on his door. He smiled to himself as he went to answer her knock.

He greeted her with a teasing grin. "That's an awful lot of noise for just one little girl. What seems to be the problem?"

"The problem?" Her voice vacillated between mere excitement and overwhelming joy. "The problem, Trent Nichols, is the painting that's hanging on my bedroom wall!"

He mimicked her excited tone. "Well, Cassie Brockton, what about the painting that's hanging on your bedroom wall? Is there something wrong with it?" It took all his willpower to keep from grabbing her in his arms and smothering her with a thousand kisses.

Cassie threw her arms around his neck, the total elation she felt at that moment radiated from her face and filled the room. "It's beautiful. I love it."

He wrapped his arms around her, lifted her off the floor, and swung her around as they both laughed and enjoyed their closeness. "I'm glad you like it."

"I don't just like it, I love it, but it's far too expensive a gift."

He lowered her to the floor but continued to hold her tightly against his body. "Didn't anyone ever tell you that it's not polite to discuss the cost of a gift?" He kissed the tender skin behind her ear as he twined his fingers in her hair.

She pulled back slightly, her gaze searching the depths of his eyes. "I love it so much, but I can't accept it. It's much too expensive."

"No, it isn't. In fact, it isn't anywhere near what I would like to have done. The second I saw that painting I knew it would be perfect on your wall."

"I don't know what to say." She rested her head against his chest, her arms circling his waist.

The shock hit Cassie as soon as she entered her bedroom and saw the painting hanging over the dresser. She had stood perfectly still for the longest moment just staring at it, confused about how it got there. Then she spotted the card on the dresser. With trembling fingers she had removed it from the envelope.

A beautiful painting to enrich the surroundings of the beautiful lady who has enriched my life. Trent.

He held her close, caressing her back and shoulders. "I'm glad you like the painting."

She remained in his arms, quietly enjoying the

moment of tender caring and togetherness.

After several quiet minutes, she raised her head from his chest and looked into the sky blue depths of his eyes. "You make me feel so very special."

"You are very special." He cupped her chin in his hand, tilted her head, and softly covered her mouth with his in a gentle and caring kiss.

****

The brisk bar business wasn't so hectic that Trent had any problems handling it by himself. It would only be for a couple of hours. Cassie had gone to Jake's house to check on him, bring him some dinner, and see if he needed anything else. Trent could tell Mike wanted to go with her, so he had volunteered to take care of the bar for a while.

Bits and pieces of conversation drifted in his direction, conversation that bothered him. More people speculating about the California registered yacht out of Marina Del Rey that had been docked in the harbor for several days. No one had been seen aboard, and the harbor master refused to provide any information. The mysterious yacht quickly gained popularity as a topic of conversation among the locals.

He wondered if Jake would say something to Cassie or Mike about his conversation with the harbor master. He wrinkled his brow in thought. Should he ask for Jake's discretion and possibly increase Jake's curiosity or hope Jake would allow it to drop and be forgotten?

Cassie and Mike returned to the bar. Both seemed relieved that Jake's condition wasn't very serious. He would be up and around in a walking cast with the aid of a crutch in a day or so and totally unencumbered in a few short weeks. Mike took back his bartending duties.

Trent caught Cassie before she could become involved in something else. "It's still early. Let's take a walk."

She readily agreed to his suggestion, and they strolled through town and along the harbor. He felt so comfortable with her, so relaxed and unpressured. Life on the island seemed truly idyllic, an answer to his quest. When he left Beverly Hills on his sabbatical, he didn't know what he hoped to find. He hadn't even known exactly what he was searching for. But he recognized it when he found it.

Cassie thrilled to his touch when he clasped her hand, not caring who saw them or what they thought. His warmth spread to her as he laced their fingers together. She felt so free, so open. Every hour of every day he became more and more the center of her universe. Her mind drifted to last night when they had made love. She had never had anyone make love to her with the degree of sensuality he possessed or the heated passion. The excitement still tingled through her body.

As they walked along the harbor, she pointed to the large white yacht. "There's that boat everyone's talking about. It's from California, but no one seems to know who it belongs to. It just arrived one day, and no one's been on it since. It looks like a very expensive boat. You'd think someone would be using it."

"Maybe the owner is visiting someone on one of the islands, and this was the most convenient place he could find to leave it." To her surprise, he abruptly changed the subject. "This Monday, the day the restaurant is closed—do you have any plans?"

"Other than being able to sleep in until a late hour

such as seven o'clock in the morning, nothing special."

"Good. Do you suppose I could prevail upon you to give me a tour of the island? Jake gave me an ocean going tour of the primary islands in the group. Now I'd like a land tour of this one."

"I'd love to."

"Then it's a date?" Adoration swam in the sky blue depths of his eyes as he squeezed her hand.

The heated flush covered her cheeks, and her insides trembled. "Yes, it's a date."

They slowly made their way back to her house. He walked her to the front door.

After she entered, Trent went through his own outside door into his bedroom. He turned on the bedroom light and the television to show anyone watching that he was in his room, then quickly exited through the door leading to the rest of the house.

Stepping into the hallway, he called her name. Receiving no answer, he ascended the stairs toward the light, thinking she might be in her office, absorbed in some business matter. When he reached the top of the stairs, he immediately spotted her sitting on the edge of her bed staring at the painting. A soft smile turned the corners of his mouth as he watched the glow of happiness radiating from her face. He entered her bedroom.

Her eyes never left the painting as she spoke to him in hushed tones, hushed, yet conveying her enthusiasm. "It's such a beautiful painting. I can't believe it's really mine. It has the look and feel of a Monet." She turned her head toward him, her soft words showing the depth of her emotion. "Don't you think so?"

He sat next to her, wrapped her in his embrace, and

pulled her to him. "Yes, I do. The colors first attracted me, then the resemblance to Monet's work kept my attention. He's my favorite artist, too."

She rested her head against his shoulder and let out a sigh. "You really shouldn't have done it. I feel very guilty about keeping it, but at the same time, I couldn't bear to part with it."

"There's no reason for you to feel guilty. I bought it for you because I wanted you to have it." He kissed her tenderly on the cheek.

"Trent?" She looked up at him, her words tentative. "You didn't do this because of last night, did you? I mean...you didn't feel obligated—"

"This has nothing to do with last night. If it will put your mind at ease, I'll let you in on a little secret. I bought the painting and had the gallery owner put it aside yesterday afternoon—before *last night*."

She again rested her head against his shoulder and closed her eyes. A smile of utter contentment curled the corners of her mouth.

****

The next two weeks flew by for Cassie and Trent, almost too quickly. A sense of foreboding occasionally came over her. Trent had made no mention of his future plans. How much longer could he stay on the island? When would he have to leave, to go back to his home? And for that matter, where was his home? She knew she would be devastated if he left, but she also knew that the time could come when he had to do just that. She did not know what to do to make sure it didn't happen...ever. She also didn't know exactly what she meant by *ever*.

Evening faded into night as the sunset gave way to

a black sky filled with a million twinkling stars. They sat on the porch swing enjoying a glass of wine, something that had evolved into a nightly ritual they both enjoyed.

"Cassie…" Trent's hesitation conveyed his nervousness. "I, uh, have some pressing matters that need to be tended to. Tomorrow morning, I'm taking the eight o'clock commuter flight to Seattle. I'll be back in two days."

Surprise at this unexpected turn of events left her almost at a loss for words. "Pressing business? What…" She stopped the question forming on her lips. "Of course."

Her fears told her he was preparing to leave the island, making arrangements for a future that would not include her. Was the painting really his way of saying goodbye? She tried to shove the irrational thoughts aside, thoughts born from her fears rather than anything tangible. A slight tremor darted through her body. Were those thoughts truly that irrational?

She had been dreading the time when he would actually leave. Maybe if she told him how she felt… Would that make a difference? Maybe then he would stay. Maybe… She shook her head. How could she do that when she didn't really know her own true feelings? Deep infatuation? True love? Or perhaps nothing more than primal lust.

She tried to clear her thoughts. She wanted him to stay because that was what he wanted to do, not because he felt obligated in some way. She didn't want to scare him off by making it seem as if she was demanding some sort of commitment. If only she knew what to do.

"That's an odd expression." He reached out and gently smoothed the frown lines across her brow. "Is there something wrong?"

She quickly recovered her composure. "No, of course not." A smile turned the corners of her mouth. "It's just that I'll miss you, that's all."

Under cover of the darkness as they sat on the porch swing, Trent pulled Cassie to him and covered her mouth with a soft, caring kiss. "I'm going to miss you, too. In fact, I'm going to miss you more than I thought possible to miss someone. Cassie, I…"

He couldn't finish his sentence. He couldn't tell her how he really felt about her, couldn't say the words. He couldn't tell her his feelings had moved far beyond just passion and desire. That he was definitely well on the way to being in love. He couldn't say it yet, not with the deception still hanging over his head. What had started as an innocent moment of holding back some information now felt more like the sword of Damocles hanging over his head.

That damn deception again. He had to clear it up. He had to be completely honest with her. He had spent many hours agonizing over it. How to tell her, how to make her understand without hurting her or embarrassing her.

And the most difficult part of all, how to tell her without driving her away from him.

He also had to make her understand his master plan, a series of events that were already in the works and would be cemented into reality over the next two days. Then, and only then, could he tackle what would undoubtedly be a major obstacle—her extremely negative opinion of his profession.

****

The alarm jarred them awake the next morning. Trent reached to the nightstand and groped for the off switch as Cassie rolled over and snuggled her body next to his warmth. "I'll work for you." He spoke in a voice still thick with sleep. "That way you can sleep a little longer."

"No, you won't." Her voice also filled with the lingering effects of sleep as she reached around and gave him a playful slap on his bare bottom.

With surprising swiftness, he grabbed her wrist. "What was that all about?"

"It's still my restaurant. So, unless you're planning to steal it out from under me, I'm the boss, and I make business decisions. You may consider that to be the equivalent of a swift kick to the seat of your pants."

His voice teased. "That's not quite accurate."

"What? Are you telling me I'm no longer the owner and operator of my own business?"

A quick frown darted across his face, then just as quickly disappeared. "That's not what I'm saying at all. It's just that—" He grinned mischievously at her. "—in case you haven't noticed, I'm not wearing any pants." His eyes reflected the still smoldering passions from the previous night's love making.

She brushed her fingertips softly across his thigh. "Trust me, I noticed."

His voice took on a husky quality as he again grabbed her hand and pulled it away from his body. "You do that again and neither one of us will be working at the restaurant this morning."

"Mmm, that's a delightful idea." She placed a light kiss on his chest, then moved toward the edge of the bed. "But not very practical."

A thoughtful expression crossed his countenance. "Sometimes you simply have to cut loose and do what pleases you rather than always being practical. Sometimes being practical isn't what's best." He spoke more to himself than to her. "But it's not always easy to know what's best."

Once again, she didn't understand exactly what he meant but knew the words came from inside him. She placed a tender kiss on his chest, then slipped out of bed.

****

Trent took the morning commuter flight from the small island airport to Seattle where he was picked up by the limo he had arranged in advance. He immediately checked into the suite at a downtown luxury hotel. The garment bag hung in the closet, the one he had Grace Edwards ship from Beverly Hills to coincide with his arrival. He glanced at his watch. He had just enough time to get a much needed haircut.

Afterward, he returned to the suite, quickly showered, and changed into the business suit. He had a meeting in fifteen minutes. He had cut his time very close.

Ten minutes later, Trent responded to a knock on the door and admitted his visitor to the suite. He extended his hand. "How are you doing, Randall?"

"Thanks to you and your impossible time schedule, I've been busier than I wanted to be." He extended a cordial smile. "I even had to cancel my golf game yesterday."

"Maybe we can get in a quick round next time I'm here."

For several hours, the two men discussed the details of Trent's business project. When they concluded their meeting, they went to the hotel's dining room and had an early dinner. They agreed to meet at Randall's office the next day right after lunch. Randall's secretary would have most of the paperwork done by then. After that, there would be a series of conference calls taking care of numerous financial details. Tomorrow would be a very busy day.

****

Cassie had become so accustomed to having Trent around that she felt lost without him. She missed sitting in the living room and watching television together, enjoying a glass of wine in the evening on the porch swing. She missed his cheery greeting to everyone, even missed the way he kept slipping into that authority mode of his, trying to take charge of things and run her business for her.

But most of all, she missed their intimate time together. She missed the feel of his bare skin next to hers, the warmth of his body, the way he caressed her, the provocative combination of the tenderness of his touch and the heat of his passion. And, just as much, she missed the moments following lovemaking when they talked quietly. Yet there were so many things she didn't know about him, so much he seemed to be hiding.

So much she wanted to know.

That thought returned her to the here and now. He was due to return in the morning. Her eyelids grew heavy as she wondered what kind of pressing business he had on the mainland and where he had gone. She finally drifted off to sleep, her dreams filled with Trent

Nichols.

****

"When is Trent coming back?" Jake sipped his coffee as he shoved his empty breakfast plate across the counter. "Not that it's any of my business—" His grin teased her. "—but you've been moping around here like a little lost puppy since he's been gone." His face took on a caring look, the concern of a dear friend. "Are things as serious between you two as I think they are?"

A thoughtful look crossed Cassie's face, then she quickly covered it with a friendly smile. "He'll be back sometime this morning."

He eyed Cassie carefully. "That's only one answer. I asked two questions. Do you think... I mean, this has all happened very quickly. Maybe you should slow down a little with Trent. I like Trent. He's certainly a very personable guy, but things just don't add up." He paused as he gave Cassie a thoughtful look. "Please don't take what I'm about to say in the wrong light. It's just that I care about you and don't want to see you get hurt by some charming stranger who's just passing through."

She looked at him curiously. "Jake, we've been very close friends from the moment I arrived on the island. I couldn't feel closer to you if you were my own father. I know you wouldn't do anything or say anything you didn't really believe." Anxiety roiled deep in the pit of her stomach, telling her she really didn't want to hear whatever he had on his mind even though he apparently wanted to share it with her.

"Cassie, honey." The words obviously came at some difficulty for him. "I think it might be a good idea for you to have Trent checked out. You know, hire a private investigator or something like that." He swallowed nervously, then continued. "I know how you feel about lawyers, but perhaps it would be a good idea if you contacted—"

The quick anger that flashed through her body said it all. "I'm surprised at you, Jake. What has Trent done to make you so suspicious?"

"It's nothing big or even anything specific. It's just lots of little things that, by themselves, don't really mean anything, but when you put them all together... Well, please be careful. I don't want to see you hurt."

"You worry too much." She poured him some more coffee, gave him a warm pat on the cheek and a confident smile, then turned to the other customers.

Jake's words, even though they were not what she wanted to hear, stayed with her. She suspected—deep inside she *knew*—Trent wasn't being totally honest with her. She hoped she hadn't gotten in over her head, that her feelings for him might be preventing her from admitting what the probable truth could be.

The morning seemed to drag by. Jake's comments kept circulating through her mind. Sometimes it felt as if hours had passed, but when she glanced at the clock she found it had only been fifteen minutes. As the morning dragged on, anxiety turned her thoughts from wondering when he would return to wondering *if* he would be back at all.

The breakfast crowd had gone, and only one customer lingered at the counter. Cassie sat in a corner booth and tried to compose her sinking feeling. He had to come back. He had personal belongings in his room. She waited. Another fifteen minutes passed. The first commuter flight from Seattle had arrived two hours ago. With a heavy heart, she went about mechanically preparing for the lunch crowd.

Time crawled by for Cassie before two o'clock finally rolled around. She put out the *Closed* sign, tended to the end-of-shift details, then went home. Once inside her house, she slumped into a chair, closed her eyes, and tried to soothe her anxiety. *Where is Trent? Why isn't he here?*

She needed to get her mind off her nagging fear. She went up to her office and opened a catalog to the page she had marked. When she had first seen the wall plaques advertised, she thought the sailing boat motif would he perfect for the bar. She had considered them for a few days and finally made up her mind. She logged on to the website and placed the order. According to the order confirmation, the plaques would arrive in seven to ten days. She was eager to hang them.

The sound of the door opening and closing grabbed her attention.

"Cassie? Are you here?"

Her heart did flip-flops when Trent called her name. Total and complete joy welled inside her. He was back—late, but he had returned. She tamped down her elation and tried to bring her soaring excitement under control.

He stood framed in the doorway. It took all her willpower to keep from throwing herself into his arms. She immediately noticed his haircut, but it was more than that. Something was different, something about his look, his expression, his demeanor. Flames of excitement burned in his eyes, flames having nothing to do with sexual passion.

He stepped into her office and immediately pulled

her into his embrace. "I'm sorry I'm late. I missed the commuter flight and had to wait for the next one." His lips brushed across her ear. "My belongings weren't scattered on the front porch. Does that mean I still have my room?"

"Another five minutes and it would have been questionable." She wanted to know so many things, but the thrill of being back in his arms pushed everything else aside. Time ceased to exist as he covered her mouth with his, a kiss conveying a feeling of soft caring and at the same time the heated passion coursing through him.

He pulled back just enough to look into her eyes. He brushed his lips against hers. A groan escaped his throat as he pulled her tightly against his body. "Oh, God, Cassie, I really missed you."

She slipped her arms around his waist and laid her head against his chest. "I missed you, too, very much."

****

Trent smoothed her mussed hair away from her face as he placed a soft kiss on her forehead. Their lovemaking had been very intense. She had given his life such purpose, such meaning, more than he ever thought possible. It had been only a couple of days, but he felt as if he had been away from her for weeks. His meetings in Seattle had run longer than he originally anticipated, causing him to miss the first commuter flight back to the island. He should have called her, let her know about the delay, but he didn't know how to explain it.

He had almost told her of his plans and his feelings as they drifted in the tender warmth after they made love. But he could not offer her a commitment until he could tell her the complete truth and could not ask her for a commitment based on a deception.

Another two weeks, at the most, and everything would be put right. He had committed a great deal of money to the project. The first phase of his plan had been completed with phase two well under way. As soon as he finalized phase two, everything could be brought out into the open and all deceptions put aside. He felt like a tightrope walker without a safety net. He had to watch every step or he might slip, and a fall could be disastrous.

A fall could be fatal.

Chapter Eight

The hours stretched into days and the days stretched into a week. Other than the fact that Trent ate breakfast at the restaurant, Cassie did not know what he did with his time while she worked, but he always appeared as soon as she finished for the day. The afternoons and evenings were always spent with him, talking, watching some television, sometimes just sitting on the porch swing in silence simply enjoying their closeness. Occasionally, they went out to dinner but usually ate at her kitchen table where they shared the cooking duties.

An air of excitement constantly surrounded him. She was acutely aware of the elation bubbling inside him, threatening to burst forth at a moment's notice. She had tried to subtly question him about it without seeming to blatantly pry into his personal business, but each time, he just gave her an inscrutable smile that widened into a Cheshire-cat grin and told her all things happen in their own good time.

Whatever had him so excited definitely connected with his trip to Seattle, but she simply could not imagine what that might be. She finally gave up trying to pry the information out of him. He would tell her when he wanted to. Funny, she felt so close to him, felt she knew him so well, even though she still knew so little about him. A strange paradox. Strange indeed.

****

"How's the leg doing, Jake?" Trent sipped his coffee as he sat next to Jake at the counter. "I see you've given up the crutch."

"Oh, it's doing just fine." He slapped his thigh and let loose with one of his jovial chuckles. "It's going to take more than a little tumble to keep me down." His expression turned serious. "I really appreciate you taking care of me like that. I suppose if I had been out there all alone I would have found some way of getting back to the dock, but it sure wouldn't have been easy."

Trent allowed a teasing anger. "If you don't stop telling me how much you appreciate me, I'm going to stop talking to you. Either that, or send you a bill for services rendered. Enough, already!"

Jake became cautiously thoughtful, then leveled a steady look at Trent. "All right. Is it okay if I tell you how impressed I was with your expert handling of my boat?"

An uncomfortable feeling welled inside Trent. Enough time had passed since that day to have allowed him a sense of security. Jake had not mentioned the exchange he had overheard nor mentioned Trent's obvious expertise in handling the boat. He thought the jeopardy had passed, that there would be nothing to explain. Now, a new set of doubts clouded his thoughts.

He tried to toss the incident away as not being relevant to anything. "I just got lucky."

Jake refused to be put off. "No, that wasn't luck. You handled it with all the expertise of an experienced seaman." He took a steadying breath while looking around, as if to make sure no one could hear them. He leaned forward and lowered his voice. "Several things have been running through my mind, more than just your handling of my boat and the conversation between you and the harbor master."

Trent's uncomfortable feeling jumped into high gear, bordering on anxiety. Apparently, Jake had not discussed his thoughts with Cassie, but neither had he dismissed them from his mind. But why had he brought them up now?

Trent tried to project a casual air while responding to Jake. "There's no mystery, I've done a turn or two on a boat in my time."

"You've been on the island for quite a while without any visible means of support. How much longer do you plan to stay? Do you intend to walk away from here as casually and unencumbered as you arrived?"

Trent shifted uncomfortably on the counter stool as he took a steadying breath. What Jake had asked was actually none of his business. Had they been in Beverly Hills in his normal surroundings, having a typical day, he would have made that fact very clear. But they were not in Beverly Hills and this was not typical of his days as a powerful, high-profile attorney. He knew Jake's motives were neither malicious nor devious, and he owed Jake the courtesy of an honest reply, as much so as possible.

Before he could answer, Jake continued. "I know it's none of my business, whatever it is that's going on between you and Cassie. But that girl's like the daughter I never had. I don't want to see her hurt by some charming drifter who's just passing through. You're hiding something, Trent. I don't know what it is or why, and you certainly don't owe me any explanations. But if Cassie means anything to you at all, don't you think you should level with her?"

Trent stood and leaned forward, his head bowed in thought and his palms pressed flat against the counter. He had been living on borrowed time knowing full well that a very real possibility existed that someone would directly confront him and demand real answers. He also knew anyone determined to discover answers could check out the registration on the mysterious yacht, learn it belonged to him, and discover where he lived and who he was. However, it appeared that no one had consciously connected his presence with the mysterious white yacht—at least not yet. Things were so close. All the pieces would soon be together and the puzzle would be a complete picture. Just another week.

Trent carefully measured his words as he raised his head to establish eye contact with Jake. "I know you have questions. I'm sure everyone does. I can't really answer them right now, but I can tell you that very soon all the questions will be answered. There's nothing sinister going on here, nothing illegal. I'm not wanted by the law or hiding out from anyone or anything. All I ask is that you indulge me for a little while longer." His manner softened. "Cassie is very important to me. The last thing I want is for her to be hurt."

Jake slowly nodded his head. "All right. Everyone's taken you at face value so far. I guess a little while longer won't hurt. But for Cassie's sake, I hope you're being straight with me."

****

The distinguished man in his late forties got out of his car and walked up the path to the motel. He had called ahead to set up an appointment with Bob

Hampton, stating the purpose of the meeting. Harold Brundage had met with Randall Davies and Trent in Randall's office in Seattle. Trent had arranged for the round trip charter flight for Harold, for a car to be available at the island airport, and had prepared the real estate broker for the meeting with Bob Hampton. Harold was ready for the brash, arrogant young man.

"Mr. Hampton, I'll get right to the business at hand. I have a client who is interested in the purchase of this property." He withdrew a contract from his briefcase and handed it to Bob. "The price you are asking is, of course, totally absurd."

Bob immediately jumped to his feet. "Hey—"

"I've taken the liberty of familiarizing myself with the contents of the lease agreement between your late mother, Bessie Hampton, and—" He opened a file folder and glanced at a document more for effect than a need to refresh his memory. "—and Sofie Daniels, the late owner and operator of the restaurant and bar located next door and owner of the house behind the restaurant, both of which are now owned by her heir, Cassandra Brockton. The lease has been inspected by an attorney versed in the ramifications of real estate law. The terms of the agreement clearly state that upon your mother's death, Ms. Brockton has one year in which to exercise an option to purchase the land containing her business and house. The purchase price for the land is set at fair market value, not the inflated price you're asking. Again, I remind you that Ms. Brockton already owns the buildings and businesses and is leasing only the land from you."

Bob sat back down. It was obvious, like Cassie, he had never really looked over the lease agreement to familiarize himself with all the conditions. The situation had apparently caught him so by surprise that it did not occur to him to ask how Harold Brundage had obtained a copy of the lease.

"Now, Mr. Hampton, your asking price is certainly far and away above fair market value for the land attested to by the appraisal commissioned by my client. I have a contract here that offers you a fair price based on that appraisal. You surely must know that without the income from the lease and the actual real estate the restaurant and house occupies, what would be left to you is some land with value and a motel of virtually no market value without the expense of serious renovations and updating to make it competitive in the market place. And without the consent of Ms. Brockton, you aren't able to sell the parcel of land she leases."

Bob tried to recover his composure, his arrogance on full display. "Oh, yeah? Well, all I have to do is wait out a few months and the year will be up and she'll have to pay what I ask if she wants to buy the land."

Harold smiled solicitously, bordering on condescending. "Mr. Hampton, if you turn down my client's offer, it will be very foolish of you to assume that Ms. Brockton will remain in the dark about the full implications of her lease agreement. In fact, I wouldn't be a bit surprised if my client decided to enter into a business arrangement that would provide her with the means to immediately exercise her option, which will leave you with nothing to sell but half the land to someone who would want to tear down the motel and build something else, perhaps more luxury waterfront condominiums."

Bob looked at the contract in his hand. "This says the buyer is something called T.A.N. Inc., a Washington corporation headquartered in Seattle." He shook his head as a moment of confusion crossed his face. "What type of a company is this? What do they intend to do with the property." Bob's confusion turned to a scowl. "Probably level everything and build those luxury condominiums you mentioned."

"Of course, Mr. Hampton, you could challenge the conditions in court, but that would leave everything tied up for possibly years and stick you with astronomical legal fees."

In a final attempt at bravado, Bob glared at the real estate broker. "Tell your client I'll think it over."

"That will be fine, Mr. Hampton. But don't take too long. My client is also looking at other properties in the San Juan Islands. You will note that this offer is only valid for one week. Here's my card. I'll leave the contract with you. Call me when you've reached a decision." With that, Harold Brundage rose from his chair, shook hands with Bob, and left.

Harold Brundage immediately walked next door. He entered the restaurant, sat at the counter, and ordered a cup of coffee. "Are you Cassandra Brockton?"

The question caught Cassie by surprise. No one ever called her Cassandra even though it was her legal name. "Yes, I am. Is there something I can do for you?"

"No, not really." He handed her one of his business cards as Trent had instructed him to do. "I was just next door conducting some business with your landlord. I have a client who has made an offer on the property. I thought you might be interested in knowing."

Cassie looked at the card. "Who's your client?"

"I'm not at liberty to say. I can only reveal that if Mr. Hampton accepts my client's offer, it will be a cash deal with immediate possession. At that time your lease agreement will transfer to the new owner. I expect to hear from Mr. Hampton in a few days. I'll contact you at that time."

She watched as Harold Brundage left the restaurant, then looked at his card as she shook her head in disbelief.

As soon as she closed the restaurant, she went looking for Trent, locating him jogging along the waterfront.

"Look at this, Trent." She handed him Harold's card. "This guy has a client who has offered to buy out Bob Hampton. Things could be changing real fast. He wouldn't say who his client is, but it must be some big company because he said the deal would be cash with immediate possession." She looked up at him, capturing the clear blue intensity of his eyes. "I...I wonder what's going to happen now?"

"I wouldn't worry about it if I were you." He gave her an encouraging smile as he handed the card back to her. "I'm sure everything is going to be okay. If nothing else, you'll be rid of Bob Hampton."

She frowned as she stared at the card. "He said he should have an answer very soon, maybe even in a couple of days or so."

Things were moving along just as Trent had hoped, just as he had planned. Very soon now things would be perfect, and he would be able to tell her everything—no more secrets or deceptions. Everything would be out in the open. He ran his fingertips softly across her cheek.

"Let's go on another picnic. The weather is warm, the sun is shining, the sky is blue, and all's right with the world."

"You seem to be in a very good mood. In fact, you've been in an exceptionally good mood ever since you returned from Seattle." She saw the smoldering blue intensity fill his eyes, a look she had grown to intimately know.

"The prospect of spending several hours in a secluded clearing in the woods, on a bluff overlooking the ocean, in the company of a beautiful and very desirable woman would be enough to put the most determined grouch in a good mood. Don't you think so?"

"Mmm. I like the way you think." She gave him a sly look that radiated pure sex and seduction. "Among other things."

He returned her look. "I like the way you do absolutely everything."

Cassie put together a picnic basket, and they returned to the bluff where they had enjoyed their first picnic. They spent another afternoon delighting in the opportunity to be alone.

Daylight lingered as Cassie and Trent returned to her house after their picnic. As he set the picnic basket by the front door, she glanced down the hill toward the bar.

"I think I'd better check on Mike, make sure he's not swamped." She squeezed his hand. "I'll be right back."

Trent watched as she walked down the path, then he entered his bedroom through the private entrance from the porch. His insides stirred with excitement.

Things were so close to being settled, so close to being put right. The entire future stretched in front of him, a bright new future that he had not even imagined could exist when he had stopped at the island just to do a favor for Randall Davies.

He opened the door between his bedroom and the house when he heard her enter through the front door. "How's Mike doing? Everything under control?"

"Yes. Mike said he had a happy-hour rush, but things have since settled down to a manageable roar." She slipped her arms around his waist as he enclosed her in a loose embrace. A slightly troubled look crossed her face. "I wonder what's going to happen, if someone's actually going to buy out Bob Hampton. I never really gave it any serious thought before now."

"Don't worry so much." He held her head against his shoulder as he tried to alleviate her fears. "I'm sure everything will work out just fine."

A sigh of resignation escaped her lips. "I hope so. What's that old saying? Better the devil you know than the one you don't? What if this new owner moves in and changes everything? What if it's some big company that decides to remodel the motel and add a restaurant? I'm worried, Trent. I can't help it."

He tightened his embrace. Just a little more time. That's all he needed. Just a little while longer and everything would be out in the open and done. He would be able to share all his plans with her, leaving only one hurdle, having to tell her he was an attorney with a billion dollars in assets. He knew her negative opinion of attorneys but didn't have a clue how she felt about billionaires. He placed a tender kiss on her forehead, scooped her up in his arms, and carried her up the stairs.

He placed her gently on the bed, wrapped her in his arms, and held her against his body. Nothing more. He just held her, reveling in her closeness. He felt the tension in her body, tension caused by her concern over the changes in the wind, uncertainty about what they meant, and how it would impact her.

He stroked her hair and kissed her forehead. She was so special, so important to his life. "Your muscles are tense and knotted. Try to relax. I promise you everything is going to work out just fine."

She raised her head and looked at him, her troubled eyes questioning and searching. "How can you promise me that? You don't know what's going to happen any more than I do."

His insides felt as if they were being torn apart. He wanted to ease her worries, but there were still too many loose ends that needed to be tied up in order to guarantee the outcome he wanted. "I'll make everything okay. I won't let anything bad happen to you, I promise."

Cassie snuggled into his embrace. "Whenever I'm with you I really do believe that nothing bad can happen, that everything really will be okay." She sighed audibly, and he felt the shudder move through her body. "What are your plans for the future, Trent? Do you go away as mysteriously as you arrived? I know I have no right to pry into your personal business, and I've tried very hard not to, but I really want to know. I *need* to know. Is that why you went to the mainland, to make some kind of...uh...*arrangements* for the future?"

He looked into the depth of her eyes, saw her fears, and felt her anxiety. He had to tell her something. He cupped her face in his hands, lowered his head, and covered her mouth with his—no heated passion, just a soft, loving kiss. "I did go to Seattle to make arrangements for the future, to take care of some business matters." He felt another shudder move through her body. "But I'm not leaving. I made arrangements that will allow me to stay. If you want me out of your life, you're going to have to tell me to go away."

Tears welled in her eyes, and a combination of relief and joy covered her face. He hugged her tightly against his body, rocking her gently in his embrace.

"Promise me something." Her voice quavered.

"What's that?"

"Promise me you'll never lie to me. Nothing could ever be so bad that it can't be worked out if we're just honest with each other."

A cold rush of anxiety swept through him. Technically, he had never actually lied to her, but the difference between lying and holding back the truth presented an extremely thin line. In court, he would have argued that purposely withholding information or knowingly allowing erroneous information to stand as fact showed an intent to deceive, which represented the same thing as a lie. "You're very important to me. I promise I'll do everything I can to make you happy." It was not the promise she had asked for, but it would have to do for right now.

"I've never been so happy in my entire life." Overwhelming love welled inside Cassie. It had not happened the way she thought it would. She had pictured this scene several times in her mind, and it had always been similar to what had happened when he bought her the painting—the joy and elation bubbling over from within, the unbridled excitement. The actuality, however, was much quieter. It had been soft and warm. Rather than an explosive moment in time. It had been the kind of feeling that lasted a lifetime. Somewhere in the back of her mind, the reality that he had not said he loved her tried to force its way into her consciousness, but she refused to allow it. Before she could say anything, he captured her mouth with his.

They each discarded their clothes in a heap on the floor, a rapidly escalating passion controlling their movements. He laid her back against the pillows as he smothered her with burning kisses.

Her hands feverishly stroked and caressed his hot skin as her bare legs tangled with his. They were gripped in the deepest passion, oblivious to everything except their searing desire for each other.

She had never before experienced the delights attainable at the far flung boundaries their lovemaking reached that night. Every place he touched her, everything he did—all of it provided a sensual ecstasy she had never before known. He resided at the center of her existence, the core of her universe around which everything revolved.

They lay quietly in each other's arms, savoring the delicious aura that enveloped them. Her head rested against his damp chest, and his strong heartbeat filled her with a sense of well-being.

"I'm so happy, Trent. I never believed it was possible to be this happy." She raised her head and brushed her lips against his.

She thought briefly about the future, speculating on what she hoped it would be, how their lives together could be arranged. He had told her everything would be all right, but she still had worries about the sale of the motel and the land. She snuggled closer to the warmth of his body and drifted into a contented sleep. She loved him. Nothing else mattered. Everything else could be worked out.

Chapter Nine

The next few days were filled with an expectant undercurrent of excitement, like a low level voltage surge that tingled but didn't hurt. Trent was more anxious than Cassie to hear about Bob Hampton's decision. Logically, the only smart thing for Bob to do would be to accept the offer. But one thing he had noticed about Bob was that the arrogant young man didn't display any signs of intelligence or even a moderate dose of good sense.

Cassie radiated her happiness. It showed in her every word and gesture. She seemed to be floating on air or, more accurately, on a cloud of euphoria. Berta and Charlene had both commented on it, and even Mike had grudgingly admitted that she seemed happier than usual. Only Jake seemed to be a little reticent in his attitude.

"Cassie, honey, you've certainly been in a good mood lately." Jake carefully formulated his words. "Is there something I don't know about that's causing it? Anything you'd like to talk about?"

"Jake, I'm in such a good mood that even Bob Hampton..." she glanced out the front window, "who's hurrying up the walk as we speak, can't dampen my spirit. Things have never been so perfect."

Jake swiveled around on the counter stool and saw Bob shoving through the door. As usual, the young man swaggered arrogantly up to the counter. "I just thought I'd let you know I've sold everything. I just signed the contracts and sent them back to the real estate broker. We talked on the phone. He'll have a cashier's check for me and I'll be packed and out of here by the end of the week."

Wariness quickly replaced what had been unbridled bliss. "Who's the new owner? When will they be here?"

"I guess it won't hurt anything if I tell you. The new owner is some Seattle corporation, T.A.N. Inc. I haven't any idea who they are or what they do. The broker, Harold Brundage, is handling everything for them. I imagine he'll be in touch with you." Bob looked around, as if for the last time. "Well, don't think it hasn't been fun. See ya!"

With that, Bob turned and arrogantly sauntered out the door.

Cassie looked at Jake. "I wonder what happens now." Her wariness increased. "If some big corporation is buying the place, that could mean lots of changes. That's been my biggest worry. That some company would buy up everything, then remodel the motel and add a restaurant. That would put me out of business."

"Don't you think it's time you had that lease of yours carefully analyzed? Maybe there's some clause about no competing business being allowed on the property. Bessie Hampton was a fair and honest woman. She and Sofie were the closest of friends. I'm sure there must be something in the lease that protected Sofie."

"Well, maybe Trent could look at it for me. He seems to have a real good grasp of things like this."

Jake shook his head. "I'd feel better if you had an attorney look at it. Sometimes legal wording can be very confusing and deceptive."

An involuntary laugh escaped her throat, one more contemptuous than anything else. "Legal wording being deceptive? Anything and everything about an attorney is deceptive. They can look you right in the eye, say something that sounds like one thing but actually means something entirely different, and do it without blinking."

Trent had entered the restaurant and come up behind her just in time to hear what she said. A quick hit of apprehension darted up his spine. He had planned to tell her tonight about everything. He had talked to Randall Davies and knew Bob Hampton had accepted the offer. The architectural plans for the remodeling had already been drawn up and he had the construction company standing by to start work. The remodeling would begin as soon as he turned over the cashier's check and completed the transfer of title.

"Cassie…"

"Trent!" She whirled to face him, surprise covering her face. "Guess what? Bob Hampton was just here. He accepted that offer for the property. It came from some corporation in Seattle." Her smile faded to be replaced by caution. "I never heard of them before—T.A.N., Inc. Have you ever heard of them?" Her face reflected her wariness and uncertainty.

He offered her a confident smile. "As soon as all the papers are filed, they'll probably get in touch with you." He lightly tickled his fingertips across her cheek. "Stop worrying. Everything will be fine."

She furrowed her brow in concentration. "I sure

hope you're right."

Trent glanced at the clock. "I've got some things to do. We'll talk about this tonight." He gave her hand a warm squeeze and flashed a teasing smile. "Stop frowning like that. It makes you look like you're worried about something."

Just the feel of his skin against hers, the warmth of his touch, made all her fears and worries vanish. Nothing bad could happen as long as he was there. She returned his smile and squeezed his hand. "Okay, we'll talk about it tonight." Her gaze followed him as he strolled out the door and down the front walk.

The rest of Cassie's shift passed quickly. Upon closing the restaurant, she went to her office to take care of the bookkeeping chores. When she finished with the restaurant portion of the business, she turned her attention to the box that had been delivered to her that morning. Her excitement mounted as she opened the package.

After pulling out the old newspapers that had been used as packing material, she removed the plaques from the carton, propped them up against the wall, and studied them. They were exactly the way they had been pictured in the catalogue, sailboats under full sail carved into the wood...everything she had hoped they would be and of excellent quality. She liked them very much. She gathered them up and carried them downstairs. She would ask Trent to hang them in the bar as soon as he got back. Her brow wrinkled slightly as she wondered where he had rushed off to in such a hurry.

She busied herself in her office finishing up a few details. Then she went downstairs and turned on television to catch the early evening news as she waited for Trent to return.

"Hi." Trent's greeting was casual but warm as he stood in the door separating his room from the rest of the house. Things were moving so fast now. He had spent the afternoon on the phone with his office in Beverly Hills, followed by a series of calls putting a whole new pattern of events into motion.

"Hi, yourself." Cassie proudly displayed her new acquisitions. "I ordered these for the bar. They just arrived. What do you think?"

He picked up one wooden plaque, then the other and studied them. "I like them." He flashed a warm smile as he set them on the table. "Do you want me to hang them on the wall for you? Which wall do you want?"

"I think that empty space by the front door. What do you think? Will they look good there?"

"Well..." He gave her a teasing grin and a quick wink. "This isn't exactly my normal line of work. I think we might have to negotiate a fee of some sort in exchange for this service."

A look of innocence covered her face as she batted her eyelashes. "Really? What ever do you have in mind?"

He squeezed her hand, picked up the plaques, and started for the front door. "That's something else we can discuss later."

After he left, she looked around the living room as a feeling of restlessness settled over her followed by a low level dose of anxiety. She wanted to discuss the property sale with Trent. She would show him her lease and get his opinion as soon as he returned from hanging the plaques. She went into her office to get the lease agreement from the files.

The newspaper mess cluttered the floor next to the box that held the plaques. One by one she smoothed out the crumpled pages, then folded them so she could add them to the recycle stack at the corner market.

She picked up the last section of newspaper, smoothed it out, then glanced casually at the contents. *The Los Angeles Times from last April.* She turned to the second page, then back again. *It appears to be the entertainment section. These pictures look like some kind of movie premiere or big party.*

A cold chill slowly spread through her body. One of the photographs, a candid picture of two people laughing and drinking champagne, leaped off the page and grabbed her attention. The man in the picture, the man dressed in a tuxedo with the sultry brunette dressed in the low cut gown who clung to his arm... He looked just like Trent. A hard lump formed in her throat. Her mouth went dry.

She closed her eyes. Dread jittered through her veins, fear of what the caption under the picture might say. Slowly, she focused on the photograph, then on the words beneath it. *Prominent Beverly Hills attorney Trent Nichols with his date, French actress Monique Devereux.*

Cassie's eyes filled with tears. Her body trembled. There had to be some sort of logical explanation. Maybe one of those weird coincidences of someone having the same name and bearing a resemblance. After all, newspaper photos weren't really all that clear...

Try as she might, she could not convince herself that it was nothing more than some strange quirk of fate. The rapidly sinking feeling inside her body told her the truth. Trent was someone rich and important, someone from Beverly Hills, someone who dated French actresses, someone who moved in the high social set. A hard jolt shot through her. An *attorney.* Another deceitful, lying attorney. The truth enveloped her like a cold, wet fog with long tentacles of ice reaching out to strangle the life from her. Her entire body felt numb.

It must have been half an hour before she could force herself to leave the office, the newspaper still tightly clutched in her hand. She couldn't make any sense of it. Surely, there had to be some sort of logical explanation. When Trent returned she would ask him about it. It had to be a mistake of some kind. He would have an explanation. He would clear up the confusion.

He would make everything okay.

****

Trent finished mounting the plaques on the wall. Before he could leave, he was drawn into a conversation with a couple of the local residents with whom he had formed a casual friendship over the time he had been there. He tried to get away as soon as he could. He smiled to himself as a warm feeling enveloped him. So many important plans for the future, so much to tell her, so much for them to discuss, not the least of which was finally being able to share his love with her. And it all had to be done tonight.

First thing in the morning, he absolutely had to go to Seattle. Papers had to be signed immediately, and he had to make arrangements for a cashier's check for Bob Hampton, which would require a transfer of funds from Beverly Hills. The timely delivery of a cashier's check was pivotal to the entire transaction. He already had Grace working on money arrangements on that end, but he still needed to take care of matters in Seattle, something he had to do in person. There could be no delay.

An anxious excitement pounded in his chest as he walked up the path to the house. He entered through his bedroom. He didn't see her downstairs. He quickly climbed the stairs to the second floor. A slight frown wrinkled his forehead. Her bedroom light was turned off and he didn't see her in her office.

He called to her. "Cassie…Cassie, where are you?"

"I'm here."

He turned at the sound of her voice, a sound that sent a jolt of fear up his spine. Her voice sounded flat, almost cold—devoid of any and all emotion. She stepped out of her darkened bedroom and into the light of the hall. Her face was drawn, her expression blank, and her eyes… He had never seen so much pain in anyone's eyes. His insides twisted into a thousand knots. Something was horribly wrong.

He immediately went to her, folded her in his embrace, and pulled her body against his. His voice carried all the anxiety crashing through him. "What's wrong, Cassie? Are you all right?"

She pushed against his chest. He reluctantly released her.

"It's this, Trent." Her hand trembled as she gave him the newspaper. "Can you explain this?" A flicker of hope momentarily lit her eyes. "It's some kind of mistake, isn't it? Please, tell me it's not true."

He saw the tears and heard the halting catch in her voice. An overwhelming sense of impending doom engulfed him. He took the paper from her hand and looked at it. A hard thud pounded inside his chest. He immediately recognized the photograph and the event.

His head snapped up, shock surging through his veins. Panic claimed every corner of his reality. A tiny glimmer of hope flickered in her eyes, then faded into darkness. All he saw was incredible pain.

She bowed her head and stared blankly at the floor. "I see. It's not some kind of mistake...not some weird quirk of fate." Her voice came out as a mere whisper.

The smooth, controlled manner of the experienced trial attorney disappeared. The dispassionate, analytical demeanor that usually got him what he wanted and won his cases failed to materialize. He stood in stunned silence as his world crumbled around him. He finally forced out some words. "Cassie, it's not what you think. I was going to tell you tonight, tell you everything about me, clear up all the misunderstandings."

"You promised me you would never lie to me, but you did." The pain in her voice was almost more than he could bear. "You lied to me about *everything*."

He grabbed her shoulders, tried to pull her toward him. Before he could wrap his arms around her, she shoved away from him. "I didn't lie to you, Cassie. I've never lied to you."

Cassie riveted him with a hard glare, welcoming the anger that covered the hurt, a pounding hurt she could no longer handle. "Never lied to me?" Her voice grew louder. "*Never lied to me?* Everything you've ever said to me has turned out to be a lie."

He grabbed her shoulders again. She felt herself verging on hysterics. Sobs convulsed inside her body as tears streamed down her cheeks.

"Cassie, listen to me. I never said anything about where I'm from or who I am. I never said I arrived on the ferry. That was your assumption."

She glared at him as she tried to regain control of her emotions and twist free of his grasp. "The spirit of the law, counselor, not just the letter of the law. To knowingly allow an erroneous assumption to stand as truth is the same thing as a lie. You purposely deceived me." She finally broke free and darted for her bedroom. Her parting words were barely audible. "You deceived me about everything." She slammed the door and locked it before he could stop her.

"Open this door, Cassie." He rattled the door handle. His voice grew louder, his frustration coming through loud and clear. "Open this door right now!" She didn't respond. He pounded on the door. "Are you going to open this door, or am I going to break it down?"

"Go away. I don't want to ever see you again." Her soft voice was riddled with pain.

He shoved forcefully against the door, then a second time. On the third shove, the door gave way. "I'm going to make you listen to me."

"Get out of here!" She screamed at him, her anger at full tilt. "*Get out of my house!*" He stood his ground, making no effort to leave. She seized the first thing within her reach, a book, and hurled it at him.

Trent's quick reflexes kept the book from striking its mark. Before she could find another potential weapon, he grabbed her wrist and pulled her hard against his body. He held her tightly in his embrace, pinning her arms to her sides so she couldn't break away. His mouth came down hard on hers, devouring her with an intense combination of anger and passion.

He relaxed his tight hold on her a little bit but did not release her from the heated passion of his kiss. She gradually went limp in his arms, not fighting, not reacting, and definitely not responding. He could deal with her fight and her anger, but he didn't know how to handle her indifference. He finally released her.

Her voice held no emotion of any kind. "Now, if you're through proving that you're physically stronger than I am, you can take your lies, your deceit, and leave my house—" A sob caught in her throat. "—and leave my life."

He grabbed her shoulders. "Don't do this, Cassie." His voice carried the deep emotion surging through him. "Don't shut me out. We can work this out. Let me explain. Don't close your life off from me. Please don't."

"Shut you out?" Her face twisted in anguish as she forced her words. "I willingly opened my home to you, my life to you—my heart to you." She visibly tried to contain a sob. "And in return you lied to me and deceived me. You once told me if I wanted you out of my life, I'd have to ask you to go. Well, I'm asking you—no, I'm *telling* you to go—right now. And don't ever come back."

Trent closed his eyes for a moment as he tried to compose his spiraling panic. He leaned his face toward hers, but she turned away. He took a calming breath as he tried to regain control over his scattered reality, then spoke softly in an attempt to bring some rationale to the situation. "It's true that I'm an attorney with a very successful law practice in Beverly Hills. I'm also a man who, over the last year, has grown very dissatisfied with his life. I arranged to take a three-month sabbatical from my practice and use that time to think out my future. I took my boat—"

"Your boat!" She glared at him through her tear-filled eyes. Then suddenly everything drained from her and her voice dropped to a mere whisper. "Of course! The mysterious yacht from California. The final piece of the puzzle."

Trent took another steadying breath and continued. "I took my boat and headed up the coast with no particular plan or destination in mind. A friend of mine, an attorney in Seattle, asked me to do him a favor. That's the reason I came to the island, why I was here when fate literally dropped you off that ladder, into my arms, and into my life."

He saw the look in her eyes, a distant look that told him she was not really listening to him, probably not even hearing his words. "Cassie..." It was as if she wasn't there. He tried again. "You were a breath of spring, breathing new life into my winter. I almost corrected your assumption at the very beginning, but the anger and bitterness in your voice when you mentioned your ex-husband was an attorney stopped me. I thought it was only a harmless little deception. It didn't occur to me at the time that you would very soon be the most important person in my life. I never thought the deception would get so out of hand. The last thing in the world I wanted to do was hurt you."

He tried again to enfold her in his embrace, but she stood there like a cold statue, not reacting to his words or his touch.

He placed his fingertips under her chin and lifted her face so that he could see into her eyes. She closed her eyes, refusing to look at him. "I love you, Cassie. I love you with all my heart and soul." A shudder moved through her body. "I'm sorry that I've hurt you. I can't do anything to change the past, but I can promise you that I'll do everything I can to make it up to you. I can promise you one other thing, too. I can promise you my undying love until the end of time."

Cassie finally managed to find her voice, to force out some words. How she had longed to hear him say those very words, but now it was too late, too late for everything. "Don't, Trent. Don't say anything else. Don't say words just because you think I want to hear them, that they will suddenly make everything okay. You've totally betrayed my trust and my love. Leave my house and leave my life."

She turned away from him, tears streaming down her cheeks. A gaping wound remained where her heart used to be. Never in her entire life had she felt as alone as she did at that moment, alone and empty inside. If only that emptiness would become numb. That way she wouldn't be able to feel the pain.

"I'll sleep on my boat tonight. We'll talk some more in the morning."

"No, we won't. There's nothing more to say. I could never love someone who lied to me, someone who purposely deceived me, someone who so thoroughly betrayed my trust. Make sure you take all your belongings with you right now. Anything you leave will be thrown away. Take your boat, your lies, and go. I never want to see you again."

He made one more attempt to hold her, reaching his arms out to her, but she stepped out of the way. "Please, Cassie, don't throw away our future like this."

He pleaded. "I have very pressing business in Seattle tomorrow, business that absolutely can't wait. But as soon as I get back—"

She turned away from him. "We have no future. Don't bother coming back. You're not welcome here." She could not say any more. Convulsive sobs took over her body. He placed his hand on her shoulder, but she immediately jerked away from his touch.

Trent stood quietly for a moment. "Cassie—"

"Go away. Get out of my house. Get off my island. Get out of my life—forever."

An audible sigh of despair escaped his lips. "All right…for now. We'll talk as soon as I get back from Seattle." He paused before turning away. "I love you, Cassie."

She heard him leave the room and descend the stairs. She tried to close her broken bedroom door, then collapsed on top of the bed. Burying her head in her pillow, she sobbed so hard her entire body shook. Her life was over. She would never be able to love anyone as much as she loved Trent Nichols.

When Trent reached the bottom on the stairs, he went to his room and sat on the edge of the bed. He didn't know what to do. If only he had told her yesterday, before she found out on her own. If only… He slowly shook his head. All the *if onlys* in the world could not change what had happened. He closed his eyes for a moment. He loved her so very much.

Without a shred of enthusiasm, he mechanically went about the job of gathering his belongings. He would be leaving for Seattle first thing in the morning.

He made a final check of the room. Everything was exactly as it was when he first arrived—with one exception. On the nightstand next to the bed rested an envelope and his key to the outside door. Some of the happiest moments of his life had been spent in this house.

His business in Seattle could not wait. Their entire future depended on him finalizing all the business details. Maybe a day or two apart would give her some time to collect her emotions. He left the house, hoping and praying he wasn't making a mistake. He walked listlessly toward the harbor, his heart heavy with sorrow.

Chapter Ten

Trent's night had been miserable. He hadn't been on his boat since his arrival on the island for fear someone would see him. He paced up and down the deck, went in and out of every cabin, but still felt confined. He tried to sleep, but he couldn't relax. He may have dozed off sometime during the night, but he wasn't certain of it.

He found himself in a real quandary and unsure about exactly how to proceed. He glanced at his watch. Four o'clock in the morning. He shook his head and climbed out of bed. No use trying to sleep. He was just too upset. He had to try to talk to Cassie again before he left. He would catch her before she went to work.

Somehow, he needed to make her listen.

As he walked up the path toward her house, he saw the upstairs light, telling him she was awake. If her night had been anything like his, she had not gotten much sleep. He went directly to the bedroom door entrance and tried the doorknob. To his surprise, the door opened. She had not even come downstairs to lock it. He entered the house. The envelope he had left by the bed was still there. He tried the inside door. It, too, was unlocked. He did not like that. She had been in the house alone all night with the doors unlocked. He cautiously made his way up the stairs.

Cassie sat on the edge of her bed, unable to move,

her insides empty, drained of all energy and feeling. She had spent a terrible night, tossing and turning, managing to sleep only in short spurts, and fitfully at that. She had wanted to stay in bed, stay hidden under the covers where it was safe, and not ever go out again. She finally managed to force herself out of bed so she could prepare for the day's work.

Her mind snapped to attention when she heard someone coming up the stairs. A quick ripple of fear darted across her skin.

"Cassie?"

She heard his voice. Before she could contain herself, she jumped to her feet and rushed for the door. Then she stopped as hurt and anger took over.

"If you don't get out of my house right now, I'm going to call the sheriff's office. You're trespassing." She said the words even though she knew they weren't true. He had paid for a full month to rent the room.

Her insides shivered as she watched the door swing open.

The sight that greeted Trent was almost more than he could handle. Dark circles showed beneath Cassie's puffy red eyes, her hair in total disarray. The pain on her face and in her eyes hit him like a cold stab to his heart.

"It's imperative that I be in Seattle this morning, but I don't want to go with things between us this unsettled. We're going to start with me telling you that I love you more than anything in the world and nothing you say or do can change that. Furthermore, I know you love me, too."

"I don't love you." Her voice was flat. "You lied to me. I could never love someone who lied to me. And worse than that, you betrayed my trust."

"You know that's not true, Cassie. You do love me, and I never lied to you. The only thing I am guilty of is holding back some pieces of the complete picture. That was wrong of me."

"There! You admit you deceived me."

"Yes, I am guilty of the crime of omission, but not of lying. I never meant to hurt you." He stepped closer to her, wanting with every fiber of his existence to wrap her in his embrace and never let go of her. "Every time I wanted to tell you what I had been holding back, I hesitated, not knowing how to tell you. I was so afraid I'd lose you."

"Well, it seems you don't need to be concerned about that any longer." The sarcasm literally dripped from her voice.

He reached out for her, drew her into his embrace, and pulled her body against his. He felt her muscles stiffen. "I love you, Cassie. You know that's true. No matter how hurt and angry you are right now, you know I truly love you."

Cassie quickly pushed away from the temptation of his touch. His words made sense but— No, she would not allow it. He had lied to her, deceived her. "I don't know any such thing. If you truly loved me, you wouldn't have deliberately deceived me. Just go away. Leave me alone. Leave my island."

"This isn't over, Cassie."

"You're wrong. It's over. It's completely and forever over." She barely forced out the words. "You played me for a fool. I won't allow you to do it again."

The intensity of his eyes burned into her consciousness. His gaze held her captive, and the power of his magnetic aura imprisoned her.

"No, it's not over, Cassie, not by a long shot. It will never be over. I love you too much for that to ever happen." He stood and took a steadying breath. "I have to leave now. I have appointments in Seattle that absolutely can't be postponed, business matters that have an impact on our entire future together. Let me assure you, by no stretch of anyone's imagination have you seen the last of me."

He gave her one final look of longing, then turned and left her bedroom.

****

Cassie stood on the bluff overlooking the small harbor. The stiff ocean breeze whipped her hair against her face. She hugged her arms around her shoulders as her body trembled, possibly from the cool, damp air but more likely from emotional turmoil. Tears brimmed her eyes, trickled down her cheeks, and a sob caught in her throat.

The sleek yacht made its way toward open water. She had told him to leave, told him to get out of her life forever. She did not need him, his lies and his deceit. He had deceived her about everything else. How could she believe he really loved her? Another sob caught in her throat as she turned away. She could not bear to watch any longer.

Slowly, she made her way back to her house. She had taken the cash drawer to the restaurant, leaving it for Charlene. Cassie needed to get ready for work. That would probably be the best thing for her. Work would take her mind off her overwhelming pain and her all-encompassing sorrow.

****

Cassie hurried past Jake on her way to refill coffee cups. He grabbed her arm, bringing her to a halt. Without a word, he took the coffeepot from her and handed it to Charlene. He forcefully escorted her out through the back door and up the path toward her house.

"Jake, what's the meaning of this?" She tried to wiggle her arm free of his grasp, but he held her too tightly. "What do you think you're doing?"

He let her go when they reached the front porch. "I've lived a lot of years and I've seen lots of people's pain, but I've never seen a look like the one covering your face. Now, do you want to sit here on the swing and talk or would you rather go inside?" His soft brown eyes studied her.

"Talk? I don't have time to talk. I need to be at work." She averted her gaze, unable to hold his look.

"What you *need* is to tell me what's wrong. Tell me, Cassie, why do you look like you've just lost your best friend in the whole world?" He tilted his head to one side. "Is that it? Have you lost your best friend?"

"I...I really don't know what you're talking about. Now, please, let me go back to work." She turned her head away, not wanting him to see the tears welling in her eyes and threatening to roll down her cheeks.

"We'll go inside." Jake opened the door and escorted her inside the house. "It's Trent, isn't it? What's happened? Is he all right? He's not hurt, is he?"

"He's gone." Cassie burst into tears and buried her head against Jake's chest. "I sent him away. I told him to leave and never come back."

He put his arms around her and tried to comfort her the best he could. "What happened, Cassie, honey? I thought the two of you were getting on real good. It was just so obvious how much you two cared about each other."

"You were right, Jake. I should never have trusted him. He deceived me." She looked up at him as she forced out the words. "He's an attorney, Jake. A Beverly Hills attorney. Another lying, deceitful attorney." She could not say any more as sobs wracked her body, her tears soaking into his shirt.

"And you love him." His words were soft. "Isn't that right, Cassie, honey?" He comforted her in his own awkward way. "That's it, go ahead and cry. Get it out of your system." He kept his arm around her shoulders as he steered her toward the couch in the living room. She needed to talk about what had happened. She could not leave it bottled up inside her.

He sat next to her. "Come on, now, tell me what happened."

Cassie continued to sob uncontrollably, pulling comfort from her friend's caring and concern. Jake didn't say anything. He allowed her to cry until she had no more tears to shed, then he pulled a clean handkerchief from his pocket and handed it to her.

"You stay right here. I'll get you a glass of water." He hurried to the kitchen and returned with the glass. She drank down the entire thing. "Do you feel better, Cassie? Can you talk about it now?"

She took several gulping breaths as she tried to get herself under control. Finally, in a voice quaking with the emotion, she began to talk. She told Jake what had happened the night before, told him about finding the newspaper article, about confronting Trent with the photo, asking for some explanation, hoping against hope that it was all a huge misunderstanding.

"What did he say?"

"He didn't say anything."

"Come now, Cassie. Do you mean you told him to leave and he turned around and walked out without saying anything? That doesn't make any sense. He must have said something to you before leaving."

She tried to speak between sobs. "He told me he hadn't meant to deceive me…told me he had planned to tell me everything last night…told me…" Tears trickled down her cheeks. "He told me…told me he loved me."

The sobs cut off whatever words she had left. She wiggled out of his arms, wiping the tears from her cheeks as she headed toward the bathroom.

As Cassie came out of the bathroom, Jake stepped out of Trent's bedroom and handed her an envelope.

Confused, she took it from him. "What's this?"

"I don't know. It's addressed to you. I found it on the nightstand in the guest room."

She stared at it, almost afraid to look inside. Her eyes filled with tears again as she dumped the contents of the envelope on the table.

Her eyes opened wide when she saw the money, bills and coins scattered across the table, mingled in with a couple of pieces of paper. Then she sifted through the array, separating out the money. She turned toward Jake.

"What have you got there, Cassie?"

"I…I don't know. It's money and—" She picked up one of the pieces of paper. "—and the check I gave Trent for working when Mike was sick." She picked up the other piece of paper, a note addressed to her. She sat down and read it.

My darling Cassie, I love you very much. Whether you admit it or not, you know it's true. I have pressing business in Seattle that can't be postponed, business that affects our entire future together. Otherwise, nothing you could have said would have made me leave with things so unsettled between us. The enclosed money is for Mike, the tips from when I worked that bar shift. It's rightfully his. I'll see you in a few days when I've finalized my business dealings. I love you more than anything, Cassie. You're my life. Trent.

She stared blankly at the money, not knowing what to think anymore. She handed the note to Jake.

He quickly scanned the words, then handed it back to her. "This note sounds very sincere to me. What do you plan to do?"

"Nothing." Anguish covered her face and filled her voice. "It's all over. He's gone, and I'm glad."

"You know you don't mean that. Did you get any sleep at all last night? You look terrible."

She tried her best to muster a smile. "You old smooth talker, that's just the kind of thing a girl wants to hear."

"Why don't you take a nap? Maybe things will be a little clearer after you've had some sleep. We'll talk later, okay?" He offered her an encouraging smile.

"I can't do that. I have to be at work. Charlene is there alone."

"She can handle things. If it gets too busy, she can call you. Now, you go upstairs and get some sleep."

Cassie's eyes filled with tears again as she shook her head back and forth, her confusion overwhelming. "I don't know what to do, Jake. I don't know what to think or believe."

He put his arm comfortingly around her shoulders and steered her toward the stairs. "You get some sleep. Things will be clearer when you're not so exhausted. I'll check on you later."

When they reached the foot of the stairs, she stopped and turned toward him. "You won't tell anyone about this, will you? No one needs to know how far things went. If they insist on some sort of an answer, just tell them..." Her gaze dropped to the floor, her shoulders sagging under her despair. "Never mind. It doesn't matter."

Cassie turned and slowly climbed the stairs.

****

Trent did not like leaving Cassie with things so unsettled, but he needed to make a final perusal of the architect's plans and go over construction details with the contractor. But most important and urgent, he had the final papers to sign for the motel purchase and funds to transfer for a cashier's check for Bob Hampton.

He also had Beverly Hills business to settle, things that required his personal attention. He needed to close his house and put it up for sale, pack his personal belongings and arrange to have them shipped to the island, and take care of the final paperwork so his law partner could buy him out as they had agreed during a phone conversation.

He had discussed having his administrative assistant continue to work for him on the island. Grace Edwards was a widow in her mid-fifties with no particular ties to Southern California. She had been very receptive to the idea. He wanted a clean break, wanted to sever his Los Angeles business ties and start fresh. He had three weeks' worth of work to do and was determined to get it done in one. He didn't want to be away from Cassie for longer than a week, especially with things in the precarious state that currently existed.

After leaving the island, he docked at Seattle and contacted Randall Davies. The two men finalized the paperwork on Bob Hampton's property and Trent arranged for the cashier's check. Next, he double-checked the architect's remodeling plans and gave his instructions to the contractor, making it clear they would answer to Randall Davies until Trent returned to the island.

He rented dock space and left his boat in Seattle. Then, having taken care of the necessary local arrangements, he caught the next flight to Los Angeles.

Trent leaned back in his first-class seat and closed his eyes. Images of Cassie, one after the other, flooded his mind's eye—the way her nose crinkled when she laughed, the sparkle in her green eyes when she was excited, and the fire when she was angry. There was the creamy smooth texture of her skin. And the honesty that covered her when they shared the intimacies of their love.

Their love... Everything had to work out. He was staking his entire future and everything he owned on that love.

He nervously went over a mental list of the things he still needed to accomplish. He had handled all his immediate Washington requirements, now he needed to do the same with his California responsibilities. The pressure and stress of the very tight time frame had started to wear on him. So many things to do and so little time.

He had not phoned Cassie since leaving the island.

Several times over the last three days, he had started to dial her number, hesitated, then decided against it. He craved a touch, a look, even to hear her voice, but didn't want to upset her any more than he already had. Maybe she just needed time to work it out logically rather than reacting emotionally. He desperately wanted to do the right thing and not screw it up any more than he already had. Unfortunately, he didn't know what the right thing was. Hopefully, he wasn't making the situation worse, wasn't setting it on a course that could never be reversed.

And it wasn't just Cassie. He owed explanations to Jake, Mike, and the others, everyone who had accepted him at face value.

He glanced at his watch. He should be landing in Los Angeles in about half an hour.

****

One day led into another. They all seemed the same to Cassie. She mechanically progressed through her daily functions—working, sleeping, and eating only because Jake made sure she did rather than her actually being hungry. Work seemed to be her only solace. The time she spent in the restaurant and bar allowed her to momentarily set aside her pain. But alone at home, she suffered the worst time of all. She saw Trent's face, heard his voice. His imagined presence haunted her every move.

Now that she had been given a few days to reflect, time to get past her initial shock, followed by hurt and anger, she had to admit the unfairness of her accusations. Jake had been right. She had a definite blind spot where attorneys were concerned. Maybe her initial outburst about attorneys did give him a valid reason for not telling her, for concealing his occupation. She wanted to believe him, wanted it to be so. But why hadn't he called? True, she had insisted he get out of her life for good and forever. But still...

Confusion ran rampant. Each day proved to be worse than the previous one. Time wasn't healing her pain. It only took her anger and turned it into more pain. Somehow, life would go on. But how?

Cassie looked out the window and saw two men coming up the walkway to the restaurant. She didn't recognize either of them, but they each had purposeful looks on their faces.

"Miss Brockton?" The man in the business suit extended his hand toward her. "My name is Randall Davies. I represent the new owner of the property."

Anxiety knotted inside her stomach. The moment she dreaded had finally arrived. She didn't know what was in store for her now that the sale had been finalized. Trent had told her not to worry, that everything would be all right. Maybe it would have been, but now that he was gone...

"The new owner will be doing some extensive remodeling of the motel, which includes plans for expansion, starting immediately. This"—he indicated the man with him—"is Steve Alexander. He's the contractor on this project. His company will be doing the construction work." Steve and Cassie each silently acknowledged the other's presence as Randall continued. "The owner's intention is to keep the motel open all year. There will be a resident manager—Grace Edwards. She'll be arriving in a few days.

"This new owner..." Cassie's voice betrayed her trepidation. "If he has a resident manager, apparently he doesn't plan to run things himself. Will he be making an appearance? I'd like to meet him since he now owns the land under my business and house."

"He should also be making an appearance in a few days. He had originally planned to be here today, but business matters delayed him."

"What kind of company is—" She searched her mind for the name Bob had given her. "—is T.A.N., Inc.? What do they do?"

"It's primarily a holding company for my client's Washington interests."

"Why would this big corporation be interested in a little motel on this island? What do they plan to do with it? What does the remodeling consist of?"

Trent had warned Randall of Cassie's specific concern. "Don't be alarmed, Miss Brockton. The new owner is fully aware of the business situation as it currently exists. He has no intention of interfering with your livelihood. In fact, I believe his intention is to enter into a business arrangement with you whereby motel guests can avail themselves of your services as part of their stay."

"Who is this person? What's his name?"

"I'm not at liberty to divulge that information at this time. I can only assure you that you have no cause for alarm in this matter." Randall Davies glanced at his watch, then turned his attention to Steve Alexander. "It's getting late. Let's do a survey." He turned back toward Cassie and handed her his business card. "If you have any problems or additional questions, please feel free to call. It was nice meeting you, Miss Brockton. I'll be in touch. Goodbye."

She watched the two men head next door to the

motel. Bob Hampton had moved out two days ago. This now made everything official. Bob was out and the new owner was in. A resident manager probably meant the new owner would not be around very much. If he didn't have any personal attachment to his new business, did that mean he would be indifferent to problems that arose from his business decisions? And what kind of woman was this Grace Edwards? Where did she come from?

All Cassie had were questions, but no one seemed to be giving her any answers.

Chapter Eleven

Trent vacillated between pleased and impatient. Although he had convinced himself he could get everything done in a week, it represented an impossible time frame. As soon as he hit the traffic and congestion of Los Angeles, he knew he had made the right decision. He wanted to get back to the island as soon as possible.

To return to Cassie.

Grace Edwards had been pleased with Trent's final suggestion on how things could be handled. He really did not want to lose her. In addition to being a first rate administrative assistant and an efficient office manager, she was fully qualified to be a paralegal if she chose to take the test. She also had a brother who owned three motels, so she was fully conversant with the hospitality industry. He had no desire to be confined to the day-to-day running of the motel. Grace would be someone he could trust. By including the manager's apartment as part of the deal, she would have a free place to live. It was a good arrangement for both of them. He even offered to pay the costs of her becoming certified as a paralegal in Washington State.

Settling his financial matters—making arrangements to sell his house, transferring banking and investment interests, having his belongings stored in Seattle until he knew exactly where to have them shipped, having his vehicles transported, and wrapping up the final loose ends at his Beverly Hills office—was all taking more time than he had originally allotted. He was anxious to get back to Cassie, but he had to take care of business first. He didn't want to have to travel back to Los Angeles in order to wrap up any remaining loose ends.

****

Cassie kept a watchful eye on the progress of the construction. Judging from the size of the crew, the new owner planned more than just a little cosmetic remodeling. That attorney, Randall Davies, said there would also be some expansion, but he didn't say exactly what that included.

All the construction activity seemed to be good for her business. In addition to the construction crew eating at the restaurant and stopping in at the bar for a few beers after work, the locals spent more time in the bar indulging their curiosity about the construction. The large parcel of land allowed for considerable expansion, new construction in addition to renovation of the existing buildings.

Each day, she anxiously watched the harbor for any sign of Trent's return. Each day, she jumped every time the phone rang. Each day, she felt more lost and alone. Each day, her despair increased as she wondered if he would ever return. Her anger had totally disappeared, leaving only despair and the fear she had driven him away for good.

And the nights were even worse, almost unbearable.

Jake sat with her one day on the porch swing as they drank their early morning coffee. He pointed toward the motel. "They've sure been working fast. It's amazing how much they've accomplished in such a short time. Have you seen exactly what they're doing over there? They're doubling the size of the motel in square feet but only adding half again as many rooms. Each existing room is being enlarged and completely upgraded. They're adding a large hot tub and swimming pool that can be used year-round, glass-enclosed in winter. The only thing I don't understand is the office-like complex that's being added on the other side of the motel lobby. It has a separate entrance from the outside in addition to a door off the lobby. It doesn't seem to have any purpose that I can see."

"Someone is sure spending a lot of money. It's a good location. If they make everything really first class without raising the rates too much, they should be very successful." A sigh of resignation escaped Cassie. "I hope Randall Davies was telling me the truth when he said the new owner didn't plan to interfere with my business operation. I took that to mean he would not be adding a restaurant or bar as part of the remodeling."

"I wouldn't worry if I were you, Cassie, honey. I haven't seen anything that looks like that type of expansion. I think it's going to be okay."

She offered him a brave smile. "I'm sure you're right. Now, I've got to go to work." She gave him an affectionate kiss on the cheek. "You're a dear, Jake. I don't know what I'd do without you."

Two o'clock finally arrived, and Cassie prepared to close the restaurant when an attractive, gray-haired woman in her fifties carrying an attaché case entered through the front door, her manner very businesslike as she walked directly toward Cassie. "Miss Brockton?"

"Yes, I'm Cassie Brockton."

The woman offered a friendly smile and held out her hand. "I'm Grace Edwards, the manager of the motel. It's a pleasure to meet you."

Cassie tentatively returned her smile and accepted her handshake. "Yes, Randall Davies mentioned your name and said to expect you."

"Things are very rushed at the moment and time is of the essence so, if you'll please forgive the abruptness, I'd like to get right down to the business at hand. We can get better acquainted at a later date. Perhaps over a glass of wine."

A hint of wariness darted through Cassie as she indicated a booth where they could sit and talk. "Of course, right this way." She locked the door and put out the *Closed* sign, then joined her visitor in the booth.

Grace opened her attaché case, withdrew a legal document, and handed it to Cassie. "This is a proposed agreement between the corporation and you that would allow motel guests the convenience of charging food and beverage to their room and paying the entire bill at one time upon checkout."

Before Cassie could express her doubts and reservations, Grace continued. "As you can see, the corporation would reimburse you for the charges in whatever time increments would be convenient for you—weekly or monthly in lump sums or, if you would prefer, at the time that particular guest checked out. If you'd rather, the corporation would be willing to reimburse you on a daily basis as you incurred the expense rather than having you wait until the guest checked out and we were paid. However, that would require some type of computer system between your establishment and our accounting system so that the charges could be maintained current at all times. The corporation is willing to help you install such a system. I'll leave this document with you so that you may look it over. If you have any questions, don't hesitate to ask. I'll be next door."

Grace stood and shook hands with Cassie. "It was a pleasure to meet you, Miss Brockton. I look forward to a smooth and mutually beneficial working relationship."

Cassie watched Grace leave, then turned her attention to the document in her hands. An incredible feeling of relief settled over her. The new owner was not going to add a restaurant. If she had a contract with the corporation to provide food service, then maybe she could trust that she would be paid. It sounded okay on the surface. She even allowed a thought to expanding her own business, perhaps adding some employees and staying open for dinner.

She glanced around the interior of the restaurant with a critical eye, seeing it in a different light. Maybe even spruce up the restaurant and bar a little. Perhaps she could talk about a little remodeling with Steve Alexander when he stopped in the bar after work, possibly get a feel for what it would cost to make some changes. She would read the contract later but didn't want to sign it until she met the new owner.

****

In addition to Grace Edwards, Trent had one more person he wanted to relocate to the island. He needed to take care of Chad Willett and the island would be the perfect place for him.

Chad's mother had been Trent's housekeeper from

the time Chad was one year old. The boy's father had died when Chad was five. At that time, Trent moved Mrs. Willett into his house as a live-in housekeeper. The boy grew up in his house. Mrs. Willett had died the previous year, just two weeks before Chad graduated from high school.

Chad's teen years had not been easy. Living in Trent's house meant Chad attended Beverly Hills schools starting with first grade all the way through high school graduation. Unlike the other kids at Beverly Hills High School, he did not have a new car, all the latest electronic devices, and lots of spending money. He had been in and out of various scrapes with the law, nothing serious...so far. But trouble nonetheless.

The one thing that seemed to really interest Chad was Trent's boat. The boy had taken it upon himself to learn as much about boats as he could. Trent had paid for him to take lessons on how to navigate at sea and how to operate a boat the size of his. He had also seen to it that Chad took a Coast Guard safety class. The boy had not disappointed him. He had eagerly tackled everything connected with the operation of Trent's boat.

Trent had promised Mrs. Willett he would see that Chad had guidance in his life and wasn't left to flounder. Trent made it a point of attending Chad's high school graduation so the boy wouldn't be the only one without someone there, then put him on the payroll as an employee while insisting that he continue to live in Trent's house. Chad's duties included taking care of the boat, maintaining the pool and hot tub at Trent's house, doing yard work, running errands at his law office, and whatever else Grace needed done.

Trent didn't need a gofer. He was not the type of man who expected people to be at his beck and call. What he did need was to make sure Chad had a clean and safe place to live, proper food, decent clothes, and adult supervision. He had offered to pay for Chad's college education, but the boy had declined the offer. He said he didn't want to waste Trent's money, maybe later when he decided what he really wanted to do as a career. Over the years, Trent had become more of a father figure for Chad than merely his mother's employer.

With Chad, it always came back to the boat. That was his great love.

Trent stood at the opened French door leading from his home office to the deck that extended across the entire back of the house and out to the pool and hot tub. He watched Chad skim the leaves off the pool's surface.

"Chad, as soon as you finish that, I want to discuss something with you."

"Sure thing, Trent. Give me about five minutes to finish here."

Trent sat behind his desk and organized some photographs Grace had emailed him that morning showing the progress of the construction. A few minutes later, Chad entered the study from the deck.

He shot a quizzical look at Trent. "What's up?"

"I want to discuss your future. As you know, I'm closing up everything in Beverly Hills—selling this house, selling my half of the law practice to my partner, and moving all my business operations to Washington State, specifically to the San Juan Islands off the coast."

"Yeah, the movers have been packing things for

the last three days."

"I've been giving a lot of thought to you and your future. For the last year you've been working for me. It's been a job that provided you a place to live and some money in your pocket. You've done a good job and have proven yourself dependable, but what you've been doing is hardly a career builder with any room for advancement."

He could tell he had Chad's full attention by the way the boy leaned forward in his chair. "Well, yeah...I've kinda been wondering what I was going to do when you left."

"I want to offer you a situation that I think will be advantageous to both of us. I'd like to move you to the island. First, you need to understand that we're not talking Hawaii with its large metropolitan area of Honolulu, no quintessential tropical paradise with swaying palm trees. I'm talking about an island far removed from all the activities you're accustomed to here in Southern California. It's also removed from the day to day activities in major cities such as Seattle and elsewhere on the mainland. The San Juan island chain makes up San Juan County. The general population of the county is approximately eighteen thousand with four main islands. The town I've established as my new home and corporate headquarters has a population of about two thousand five hundred people. There's a healthy influx of people during the summer, but winters are pretty quiet. The winter weather is also a lot more severe—and definitely colder—than Southern California."

A teasing grin pulled at the corners of Chad's mouth. "You mean they don't have bumper-to-bumper traffic jams and smog?"

The spontaneous laugh escaped Trent's throat. "That's one way of putting it." Then his manner turned serious again. "You would be employed by my new Washington corporation. Initially, your primary duties would be to take care of the boat, as well as the pool, hot tub, and landscaping at the motel—pretty much what you're doing now. You'd also help out at the motel with whatever Grace needs, which could include learning to handle the registration desk and interacting with the motel guests. As I said, that's for now. My long range thought for you is to be in charge of the boat as a charter operation—sight-seeing tours, whale watching trips, that type of thing. It's not a fishing boat, and I don't want to turn it into one. What do you think? Does that sound like something you'd be interested in doing?"

The smile that spread across Chad's face said it all. "You'd let me do that? Handle the boat on my own with sight-seeing tours and whale watching trips?"

"That's on down the road, probably at least a couple of years away. There's a lot of work that needs to go into setting up that type of an operation, not the least of which includes doing some remodeling on the boat, getting it certified for paying passengers, and you going through the training for your proper licensing. It's going to take a lot of your time for studies in addition to maintaining a work schedule. You'll also need to be well versed on local history and geography as well as knowledgeable about both the humpback whales and Orcas, dolphins, and sea life in general as it applies to the area as well as birds and other wildlife so you can answer people's questions. It will mean a lot of work and dedication on your part. Does it still sound like something you'd be interested in?"

Emotion welled in Chad's eyes. "You've been real good to me, Trent. Both me and Mom. I know when I was younger I wasn't as appreciative as I should have been, and I'm real sorry about that. I promise you, if you let me do this, I'll work real hard and make you proud of me."

Trent extended his hand toward Chad. "Then we have an agreement." They shook hands. "I want to be out of here day after tomorrow, first thing that morning. You'll fly out with me so pack your stuff and handle whatever you need to do before moving to Washington."

He leaned back in his chair after Chad left the room. All he could think about was Cassie—seeing her, hearing her voice, touching her, holding her. He had missed her so much. It had been a very long and busy two weeks. Just the rest of today and tomorrow, then he'd be on his way back to the island.

****

One day merged into another for Cassie. The two week mark had come and gone without any word from Trent. With the construction going on next door, a constant flurry of activity seemed to surround her. Her days should have been filled and busy, but they weren't. The people closest to her tried to cheer her up. Even Mike made a valiant attempt at being upbeat. Everyone knew, without Jake telling them, that the source of her obvious sorrow was whatever had happened to cause Trent to leave so suddenly without even saying goodbye to anyone.

Cassie had pretty much kept clear of the motel.

Once she had ascertained that there wouldn't be a restaurant or bar at the motel, her despair had prevented her from being too curious. But now that the construction seemed to be far enough along to clearly see how everything would be laid out, she took a few minutes to wander next door. She spotted Steve Alexander and walked over to where he was studying the blueprints, in particular a section having to do with the glass-enclosed hot tub and swimming pool. Architectural drawings spread across a large worktable.

She picked up a drawing and unrolled it. She stared blankly for a moment, then shock hit her as she realized what it depicted. She held an artist's rendering of how the completed project would look. It showed the front of her restaurant remodeled to match the look of the motel and a physical connection between the buildings, an enclosed walkway that appeared to make her restaurant part of the motel.

"What is this?" Her sharp question cut into Steve Alexander's concentration.

Steve looked up. The confusion cleared from his face when he saw what she held but was quickly replaced with wariness. His hesitation before speaking set off alarm bells.

"That's just one of the artist's renderings that came as part of the architect's package. It's not part of what we're working on. We don't have any construction plans that go with that drawing."

"But why is it here? Why would the drawing have even been made? My restaurant is a separate business, not part of the motel."

"Gee, I don't know, Miss Brockton. Maybe Grace can answer your question. She's in the lobby."

Cassie rolled the drawing, tucked it under her arm, and hurried off. She did not know whether to be angry, upset, or worried. She did not like the look of this, the direction it seemed to be taking. She quickly found Grace Edwards. Without saying anything, she unrolled the drawing and spread it out in front of Grace, then looked at her questioningly.

Grace frowned as she stared at the drawing. "That shouldn't be here. It's just a drawing the artist did from photos of the motel. One of the photos of the front of the motel was taken from an angle that inadvertently included your restaurant. The artist didn't understand that your business is separate from the motel and not part of the corporation." She smiled as she rolled up the drawing. "Please don't let this upset you."

An inner sense tugged at Cassie's consciousness. Why did it seem that everyone was so concerned about her being upset? Why would these strangers have any knowledge of her history with Bob Hampton or the particulars of her lease arrangement? Maybe Grace considered their conversation over, but she did not. "Who or what is this T.A.N., Inc.? I haven't signed that agreement yet and won't consider it until I've had an opportunity to meet the new owner."

"The owner should be here sometime tomorrow. He arrived in Seattle this morning. I'm sure he'll be in touch with you as soon as he's here."

****

Chad docked the boat at the island's harbor in the pre-arranged prime space reserved with the harbor master. Trent was very pleased with the way the boy handled everything. As soon as the boat had been secured and hooked up to dockside facilities so they could stay on it, Trent sent Chad on to the motel. "Tell Grace I'll see her in a little while. I have a few things I need to take care of first."

Nervous tension settled in his stomach, the moment finally at hand, he would see Cassie and talk to her for the first time in almost three weeks. He had missed her more than he thought possible to miss someone. But uncertainty continued to plague him concerning what her reaction to his return would be. Hopefully, the separation had been beneficial, allowing time for her to sort out her anger and hurt from her love. He took a calming breath to steady his nerves, then changed into a custom-tailored suit. After making a last-minute check of the papers in his briefcase, he left the boat and headed to the motel. He went directly to the area where Grace had set up the temporary office.

She looked up from her work and gave him a weary smile. "Am I glad to see you."

"How are things coming along?" He looked around at the activity. "Is everything on schedule?"

"We're a little bit ahead of schedule." She handed him a status report, the type of rundown he liked—a quick statement of exactly what had been accomplished since the last report, what was left to do, and closing comments regarding any related incidents or problems. Trent quickly scanned the report and knew exactly where things stood.

A frown wrinkled his brow as he got to the bottom of the report. Cassie had come across the drawing showing the motel and restaurant as part of the same complex. He looked up at Grace. "What did she say?"

"She was understandably upset. She's most anxious to meet the new owner, says she won't consider the room charge agreement until she does."

Grace shot him a look, a combination of longtime employee who knew how far she could push the boss and motherly concern. "She's a very nice girl, Trent, and she's extremely worried about what's going on here. Don't you think you should be straightening out this mess you've created instead of talking to me?"

It was after two o'clock. The *Closed* sign had been posted at the restaurant. Trent entered through the bar, immediately spotting Jake and Mike who were engaged in conversation. He didn't like the nervousness and uncertainty churning in the pit of his stomach. Trent Nichols was a man with a commanding presence, accustomed to being in control, to having all the facts at hand, and knowing exactly where everything stood. He took a steadying breath as he tried to swallow his unaccustomed and growing anxiety.

Mike saw Trent first. His conversation stopped as he stared. Jake turned to see what had grabbed Mike's attention. Trent acknowledged both men in a friendly but businesslike manner.

It was Jake who came out of his stunned silence first. He jumped up from the bar stool and ushered Trent into a quiet corner. His voice dripped with irritation. "Just where the hell have you been for the last nineteen days?"

Trent had not been sure what type of reaction would greet him, but this certainly was not one of the options he had considered. He glanced back at Mike, who stared at him with more curiosity than anger. Trent returned his attention to Jake.

"I've been taking care of business, making arrangements so I could come back here and be able to stay." His voice softened as he glanced toward the restaurant. "How's Cassie doing?"

"Almost three weeks and not a word from you. How she's doing depends…are you here to stay or just passing through again? I think she's gotten past the fact that you're… How did she put it? Another lying, deceitful—"

Trent held up his hand and smiled. "Yes, she shared that opinion with me—several times." The smile faded from his face. She had obviously told Jake about his true identity. He wondered who else knew. "How much did she tell you…tell everyone?"

"Well, there isn't any *everyone*. There's only me, and I think she probably told me pretty much all of it. She let me read the note you left."

Trent stared at the floor. "I see." He paused for a moment to collect his thoughts, then looked at Jake. "I owe several people an explanation, but first I want to see Cassie. Where is she?"

"She's home, probably in her office."

"I'll see you later, Jake." With that, Trent left the bar through the back door and walked up the path toward Cassie's house.

****

Cassie sat at her desk finishing up the daily bookwork from the restaurant. For the past hour, her stomach had been doing flip-flops as a nervous tremor darted back and forth through her body, more like a premonition of something, but she didn't know what. Too many things were happening, much too unsettled, the day more than half over with no sign of the new owner.

She leaned back in her chair and closed her eyes. A

vivid image of Trent immediately appeared on the screen of her mind. She had sent him away, insisted he leave, told him to get out of her life, and emphatically demanded that he never come back. She had refused to listen to what he tried to say. She had been hurt and angry. She had felt betrayed.

Now, more than anything, she wished she could take back those awful and hurtful words. He had said he would return in a few days, but something had obviously happened to change his mind. Her heart ached as she tried to come to terms with the growing awareness that he might have taken her words to heart. That he could truly be gone forever.

With a heavy sigh, she rose from the chair and went downstairs. She paused at the door of the guest room, then went inside. She stared at the bed and wondered if she would ever be able to stop loving him. The doorbell startled her out of her moment of sorrow and despair, one combined with a little bit of self-pity.

Trent.

The afternoon sun glinted off his dark blond hair. His eyes seemed a much brighter blue than she remembered. He looked very impressive in his light gray custom-tailored suit and so very handsome. He appeared every bit the successful, high powered attorney from the top of his expensively styled hair to the bottom of his Italian loafers. Her heart pounded in her chest as he held her captive in his gaze. Her throat tightened, and her mouth went dry. Could this possibly be real, or was it merely a hallucination conjured up from her desires and despair?

Tears welled in her eyes, threatening to spill over and trickle down her cheeks. She desperately needed to get her soaring emotions under control. She vacillated between her overwhelming joy at seeing him and her irritation with him for not contacting her even once during his nearly three week absence, a borderline anger she immediately recognized as completely inappropriate, especially since she had pointedly told him to get out of her life forever.

"They say absence makes the heart grow fonder." His voice soft, smooth, sexy, and very loving. "Is that true, or am I in even more trouble than I was before you threw me off your island and told me to never darken your door again?"

She tried to maintain a tough stance. "What are you doing here?"

"May I come in, or do you prefer to discuss our business from opposite sides of a screen door?"

He seemed almost too casual to her. She did not know quite what to make of it. "What business could we possibly have to discuss?"

"Well, for starters, I understand that you refuse to sign the agreement with the motel until you've met the new owner."

A quick intake of breath passed between Cassie's lips. Her tough attitude vanished in the blink of an eye as her insides trembled with the full realization of what he had just said. "You? You're this T.A.N., Inc.?"

"Trenton Anthony Nichols. I know it's not particularly clever, but I was in a hurry and didn't have time to do extensive research on available names before forming a Washington corporation. So, as you can see, we definitely have business to discuss." The casual manner faded, and his face became very serious.

She heard the strain in his voice and saw it etched

in his handsome features. "Are you going to let me in, Cassie, or do I need to break down another door?"

"I haven't repaired the last door you broke." She had difficulty assimilating everything. From out of nowhere he'd appeared on her porch, not as the mysterious stranger she had fallen in love with, but rather as a sophisticated, successful, high-profile attorney in a custom-tailored suit, an attorney who apparently now owned the land under her business. She didn't know what to think or feel.

Trent reached his hand out and touched the screen door with his fingertips. He had reached his limit, so near to her, yet unable to touch her. "Please open the door, Cassie. We have lots of things to talk about, much more than just business."

He saw the confusion and uncertainty in her green eyes as she hesitated. She finally released the latch on the door, then turned and walked into the living room. He entered the house and closed the door.

Trent reached out for her. He had to touch her, to feel her warmth. He had never before believed that nineteen days could be such a long time. Even though he had been extremely busy, it had seemed like several months. He turned her to face him. "I'm sorry about your door. I'll send someone over to fix it." He pulled her into his arms, his tenuous composure slipping away. "I love you, Cassie. I love you so much."

She rested her head against his shoulder and slowly circled her arms around his waist as a sob caught in her throat. "How could you keep so many secrets from me if you really loved me? People who love each other are supposed to trust each other and share, not hide things from each other. You not only deceived me about who you really are, but now I find that you're the new owner of the motel. You continued to deceive me at the same time as you were telling me you didn't mean to."

He continued to hold her in his embrace. He was not sure how to answer her. "I didn't mean to deceive you, that wasn't my intention. I'm accustomed to making decisions in a hurry and acting on them. It's the way I've always done things. And this entire business situation, for me, literally came out of nowhere. It exploded in my mind with time being of the essence. There were so many elements, especially handling Bob Hampton as quickly as possible. I had to act immediately to nail everything down. I'll have to learn to handle matters differently now—with your help. I want you to know everything. I don't want there to be any secrets between us."

She trembled against him. "I don't know, Trent. I don't know what to think or what to do. You left me a note that said you'd be back in a few days, and that was the last I heard. The last nineteen days have been miserable. You didn't call like you said you would, not even once."

Chapter Twelve

Trent's voice lowered to a whisper. "Every day, I'd start to dial your number, then I'd stop. I didn't know what to say. I didn't want to take a chance on making you even more angry by trying to explain things over the phone from twelve hundred and fifty miles away that really needed to be addressed in person. I still had too many loose ends to tie together."

He tightened his hold on Cassie, squeezing her so hard she thought he was going to cut off her breathing. "I love you, Cassie." His words held more emotion than she thought possible for anyone to convey with mere words. "You're my entire life. Nothing else matters. Without you, I have nothing. All the material possessions I've accumulated don't mean anything without someone to share them with, and you are that special someone."

She raised her head and looked into the blue fathoms of his eyes. "I don't even know who you are. I thought I knew, but now I realize I don't."

"Yes, you do. Just because you didn't know what I am doesn't mean you don't know *who* I am. I'm the same man who was here before. Maybe the clothes are different and the background isn't what you thought, but the man's the same. You're my life, Cassie. You're the most important thing in my world."

They stood for a silent moment, then he released

her from his embrace. Moving quickly, he cupped her face in his hands and lowered his mouth to hers. It was there, all of it. All the passion, all the fire, all the gentle caring, all the tenderness...all the love. So many emotions and feelings magically combined into one kiss.

A swirling cloud of euphoria enveloped Cassie the moment his mouth came in contact with hers. She loved him so much. Just his touch made her lose all concept of reason and logic. Her last conscious thought sent up a silent prayer asking if he had returned with the intention to stay permanently.

"I've missed you so much." His breathless words tickled across her ear. His lips left fiery trails as his hot kisses smothered her.

Cassie tried to regain her senses, to take control of a situation rapidly spiraling beyond what either of them had the ability to contain. "Please, Trent..." She tried to pull away from him. "Don't do this. I..."

Reluctantly, Trent loosened his grip on her. He threaded his fingers in her short blonde hair and held her head against his shoulder. "I'm sorry, Cassie. I shouldn't have done that, but I couldn't stop myself. It's just that I love you so much."

"What's happening?" She looked at him with questioning and wary eyes. "Explain to me what's going on, what you're doing, what your plans are. I've been in such a state of turmoil, and I'm so confused."

"I know, and I'm sorry. I didn't mean for things to upset you. It's just that my plans formulated so fast, took shape so rapidly. Everything moved so quickly with super critical timing. When I left Beverly Hills on a three-month odyssey, I had no idea anything like this would happen. The last thing I expected was to stop here and have someone as incredible as you literally fall into my life and change it forever."

Trent tried to get his thoughts together in some kind of logical order. "Things happened so fast after that. Suddenly, my head filled with thoughts and plans, plans that required a lot of ground work to bring them to fruition. For the first time in a long while I found possibilities that excited me. I felt alive again, totally invigorated. Life still had meaning, still held challenges. I had to make decisions, and I had to make them quickly. Everything I've done, all the plans I've made for the future have been with you in mind."

"If you were making plans for a future that included me, don't you think you should have consulted me?"

He allowed a slight smile to curl the corners of his mouth and a sigh to escape his lips. "You've got me there. You're absolutely right." He kissed her tenderly on the forehead. "Am I too late?"

"I…" Her words were hesitant. "I don't know."

His arms tightened around her. "Don't say that, Cassie. I love you and you love me. That's the bottom line. Everything else can be worked out, starting right now." He released her from his embrace, placed his hands on her shoulders, and captured her in the magnetic pull of his gaze. "The first order of business is for me to dispel any worries and concerns you have about what's going on and how it relates to your business." He took her hand, led her over to the couch, and sat down.

"Now, I'll start by telling you what I have planned. Feel free to interrupt me at any time if you have any questions." For the next two hours, he explained to her everything he had done, all the preparations he had made so he would be able to make a smooth transition from Beverly Hills to the island.

"You haven't said anything. Don't you have any questions? Have I answered all your concerns? Please, Cassie...anything that's not clear, anything I haven't explained, anything that's troubling you. Talk to me."

"I don't know. You've given me an overwhelming amount of information." She slowly shook her head. "So much you kept to yourself. I just don't know."

He took her hand and stood up, bringing her to her feet with him. "Come on, I'll give you a tour of my new office, then a tour of my boat. And then I have a present for you. Remember, if you think of any questions along the way, just ask me."

Cassie's mind whirled at the extent of Trent's plans. She still had difficulty grasping the magnitude of what he had put together. She seemed to be in a daze that she couldn't shake. He opened the front door and escorted her out onto the porch. She immediately spotted Jake lurking around the back door of the restaurant, watching the house. She turned a questioning look toward Trent.

"Yes, we had a couple of quiet words in the bar before I came up to the house. I wanted to get a feel for whether you were going to listen to what I had to say or try to toss me out on my butt. I owe Jake and lots of other people an explanation." He stopped walking, his brow furrowed in momentary concentration. "Now might be a good time. I'll take everyone on a tour of the construction and explain what it is. And by everyone I mean Berta, Charlene, and Danny, too. They were trying to be very unobtrusive but obviously hanging around the kitchen when I walked through. If you and Mike feel comfortable about leaving the bar in the hands of a few trusted customers, I'm sure he'd also like to check things out along with everyone else."

Trent asked the group to gather in the restaurant, away from the bar customers. "I owe all of you an explanation of what's going on here. First of all, I'd like to confirm what you probably all know by now. I'm an attorney and have had a very lucrative and highly successful law practice in Beverly Hills, California. The mysterious white yacht from Marina Del Rey that seemed to capture everyone's interest is back and belongs to me."

He had everyone's rapt attention as he continued. "Now for what you don't know. I am T.A.N., Inc., the new owner of the motel." An immediate buzz of surprise rose from those assembled as eyes widened in shock. "The construction currently going on serves two purposes. First, the motel is being upgraded and expanded with the intention of being open for business year-round. Second, I'm adding an office complex to take care of my other business interests since this is now my corporate headquarters. Among those business operations will be a law office for those who can afford an attorney and a legal aid office for those who have viable cases but can't afford to hire an attorney. Both offices will serve the needs of the people here and on the neighboring islands." Trent showed the group around the construction and made sure everyone met Grace and Chad.

Berta, Charlene, Danny, and Mike talked excitedly among themselves as they left the motel and went back to the bar. Jake stayed behind when Trent invited him to go on a tour of his boat along with Cassie.

Jake seemed very impressed with Trent's boat. "No wonder you were able to handle my fishing boat so expertly. If you handle this big thing all by yourself, my little boat must have seemed like child's play." He looked at her questioningly. "What do you think, Cassie? Real nice, isn't it?"

Cassie spoke softly and without emotion. "Yes, it's very nice."

Trent couldn't hide his anxiety and concern. She hadn't uttered a dozen words since they left her house. He had no idea what thoughts circulated through her mind, what she was hiding.

Jake apparently took her silence and Trent's anxiety-ridden face as his cue to leave. "Well, I've got some errands to take care of, so I guess I'll be running along."

Trent put his hands on Cassie's shoulders and guided her back inside the main cabin of the boat. "You haven't said much. What are you thinking?"

She collapsed into a chair, a quick look of despair darting across her face. "I don't know what to think. You have me so confused."

He knelt on the floor next to her chair, taking her hand in his and looking into her eyes. "I love you, Cassie, and I'm very sorry for the pain I've caused you. I know this has been a lot all at once. Have I left anything out? Do you have any questions I haven't answered? Is there anything you want to know or are unsure about?"

"I don't know, Trent, I just don't know. So many things..." The tears welled in her eyes. "So many secrets. I just don't know what to think." She shook her head. "In fact, I can't think."

He cupped her face in his hands, his gaze searching, then finally settling on her eyes. "I promise you, there will never be any secrets again—never. I love you, Cassie. Without you, my life is an empty void."

Cassie looked around the cabin, as if actually taking it in for the first time. The past few hours had been mind-boggling—so many new things, so much to digest and consider. "Where does this leave us, Trent? You're now my new landlord. I make lease payments to you each month. Why do you have a drawing showing my restaurant as part of your motel? What is our business relationship? And what is our personal relationship?" A sob caught in her throat. "And when will you decide this is tedious, that the island is too much isolation for you, and it's time for you to move on again?"

"Move on? Is that what's bothering you?"

"Well..."

"Cassie, listen to me." He rose to his feet and pulled her up from the chair. Wrapping his arms around her, he held her head to his shoulder. He spoke in a calm voice, his tone loving. "I sold my half of a very lucrative Beverly Hills law firm to my partner. I closed my house in Beverly Hills and put it up for sale. I transferred all my financial dealings to Washington banks and brokerage firms. I formed a Washington corporation to operate my business interests. I bought out Bob Hampton using a noticeable amount of my cash reserve so that finalizing the transaction would be immediate. I committed the financing to do extensive renovations at the motel. All my personal belongings are on their way to Seattle to be put in storage until I can give them an address for delivery, including three vehicles. I've relocated two of my employees here and have guaranteed them employment with my new Washington corporation. I'm going to take the Washington bar exam so I can practice law in this state. Does that sound like someone who's just *passing through*? Someone who will be gone as quickly as he arrived?"

She slipped her arms around his waist and looked into the honesty of his eyes. "What about us?" Her voice conveyed all the apprehension coursing through her veins.

"Us? I want us to spend the rest of our lives together. That's what about *us*." He kissed her tenderly on the forehead, then brushed his lips against hers. "The reason I had an artist's rendering showing the front of the restaurant and the motel as being connected was because it seemed like the logical thing for us to do with the two businesses after we were married."

Had she heard him correctly? "Did you say married?"

"Of course, married. I love you and you love me. Where else could that possibly take us?"

She wrinkled her brow in a moment of uncertainty. "Marriage is a fifty-fifty partnership. My ex-husband never understood that. Do you?"

"I've always understood it intellectually." He captured and held a moment of intense eye contact with her, a moment that made her feel as if he had reached inside her and could read her most inner thoughts. "And now a very painful lesson has opened the door to understanding it emotionally. I'm so sorry that I didn't talk to you about my plans...plans that clearly involved you. Plans that should have been *our* plans. Please say you forgive me."

"Do you promise that you won't try to make my decisions for me? That we'll work out problems together."

"Absolutely." He lowered his head and captured her mouth with a loving kiss. "We'll apply for a marriage license first thing in the morning."

"Excuse me? That promise to not make my decisions for me didn't last too long."

"What?" Confusion covered his face.

"Before *we* apply for that marriage license, don't you think you should give me a chance to actually accept that marriage proposal first?"

A hint of a sheepish grin tugged at the corners of his mouth. "Please be patient with me. Apparently, I don't re-train as easily as I assumed."

He released her from his embrace, picked up his briefcase, and removed a small velvet box. He took her hand and slipped the diamond ring on her finger. "I love you very much, Cassie. Please do me the honor of marrying me."

Cassie looked at the ring, the brilliant diamond sparkling in a gold setting. She looked up into the honest love emanating from his face, then back at the ring. Her heart felt lighter than it ever had as her love for him soared. Tears brimmed her eyes again, but this time tears of joy. "It's beautiful. I love you, Trent."

Before anything else happened, he took a moment to remove a legal document from his case and held it out to her.

She stared at it but didn't take it. "Is this what I think it is? Is this—" She swallowed in an attempt to get rid of the lump in her throat. "—a...a prenuptial agreement?"

A moment of confusion crossed his face. "A prenuptial agreement? No. This is a pre-wedding present."

Cassie looked at him questioningly, then at the document. She took it from him and read it slowly and carefully. Her hand trembled slightly. "Trent?" The love she felt for him welled inside her until there wasn't any room left for anything else. "Is this what I think it is?"

"If you think it's the deed to the land your restaurant and house sit on, then you're right. That's exactly what it is. I don't want there to be any doubts, concerns, or fears on your part about exactly where things stand legally. You now own the land, which negates the lease agreement and your lease payments. It's yours, free and clear."

She looked at the ring, then at the deed again. Married! The word repeated over and over in her mind. The two of them husband and wife. She had never been as happy as she was at that moment. She slipped her arms around him, her voice soft and loving yet with just a hint of a teasing quality. "A diamond ring and a land deed... Is this your idea of how to sweet talk a girl into marrying you?"

He flashed a teasing grin. "Is it working?"

"It's a great start."

He picked her up in his arms. "Have you ever made mad, passionate love on a boat?"

"That sounds more like a proposition than a

proposal."

He whispered provocatively in her ear. "It's both."

"I accept your proposal"—she smiled seductively as she loosened his necktie—"and your proposition."

A word about the author…

I've lived most of my life in Los Angeles and earned my living for twenty years by working in television production. I was always interested in writing and dabbled at it, but not seriously. I combined my interest in writing with my avocation of photography and began doing magazine articles featuring my photographs. After selling several articles, I discovered I enjoyed the writing process as much as the photography.

My friends told me I should make use of my television contacts and write scripts. I enrolled in a screen writing class at UCLA. By the close of class I knew screen writing was not for me. The other thing I knew was that I wanted to write novels rather than magazine articles.

~*~

Visit Shawna at
www.shawnadelacorte.com
https://shawnadelacorte.blogspot.com

Thank you for purchasing
this publication of The Wild Rose Press, Inc.

For questions or more information
contact us at
info@thewildrosepress.com.